After Sixty: Going Home

May your home
(and your life)
be blessed.

Gertrude / [illegible]

After Sixty: Going Home

Gertrude Story

THISTLEDOWN PRESS LTD.

Canadian Cataloguing in Publication Data

Story, Gertrude, 1929-
After sixty: going home

ISBN 0-920633-82-X

I. Title.

PS8587.T677A35 1991 C813'.54 C91-097103-X
PR9199.3.S76A35 1991

Book design by A.M. Forrie
Cover illustration by Alicia Popoff
Typeset by Thistledown Press Ltd.

Printed and bound in Canada by
Kromar Printing Ltd.
725 Portage Avenue
Winnipeg, MB R3G 0M8

Thistledown Press Ltd.
668 East Place
Saskatoon, Saskatchewan
S7J 2Z5

Acknowledgements

"Wanted" first appeared in *Grain* magazine. "Running Hot and Cold" first appeared as "Old" in *Imagining Women* (The Women's Press, 1988). *"Alles Verrückt"* is to appear in *The Bridge City Anthology: Stories from Saskatoon* (Fifth House, Saskatoon, 1991).

The author wishes to acknowledge the financial assistance of a Saskatchewan Arts Board grant to help bring this book into being.

This book has been published with the assistance of The Canada Council and the Saskatchewan Arts Board.

For The Writer Inside:
The Dream Maker:
The Keeper of Soul who holds my life, my heart,
precariously in firm but gentle hands.

CONTENTS

Girl's-eye View, After Sixty

When I was young   and it was late September
and an early moon was out   and maybe a few stars
and I heard my Uncle Emil yodelling
above the clatter of the hayrack pounding pell-mell
down the sandhill towards our place
I left the bunting calves taking skim milk from my pail
looking surprised in the feedyard pen
while I ran to tell my mother
Threshers coming!
Oh I'm not ready! she always said
but that did not stop them from coming
harness jangling   horses coughing
the breathy whistle hooting the arrival of the steamer
(and trying hard to play our mother's name).

Our brother Rudy   got to go outside
and sit on fence rails out of the way of horses' hooves
and smell and see and taste the wheat dust and the horse sweat
and hear the dirty jokes and songs
and be sneaked widgins of tobacco from an Old Chum chewing plug.
We girls got to cut cold boiled potatoes into an iron fry pan
and slice roast beef and onions and brown bread and raisin cake
and set table for sixteen wrapping the legs in brown paper
saved from Eaton's parcels
so the men's boots wouldn't scrape the varnish
paid for hard by pounds of butter
peddled to fat women in town
who answered the door in curlers
and called my mother the Butter Woman to her face.

And when the men left   once the wheat was in
each one left a dime hid
underneath his saucer or his plate.
And we had to share with Rudy who was learning how to yodel
while my sisters washed the dishes
and my crying hands scraped plates.

GO LIKE SIXTY

"She wanders in the halls all hours of the day and night. She knocks on doors and asks what time it is twenty times a day. It's not the interruptions," said Kurt, "though heaven knows I can ill afford the time away from my research to conduct a senile old woman back to her room repeatedly in one morning. I'm sure she has family. Relatives of some sort. Why don't they put her away somewhere?"

"Where?"

"Well, you know. Somewhere. Nursing home. Care home. I don't know what they're called. Government places. Manitoba is supposed to be the epitome of socialized medicine, everybody here keeps bragging that England and Sweden and you name it come here to study the system, so surely there's a place for an old woman to be taken care of by people who are paid for it."

It was All-you-can-eat Spaghetti night at the pizza place at the local mall. I was new; Kurt knew all the angles. He'd invited me for supper "any Monday" I liked. Now I knew why: Monday was Two Eat for One Price night. Which was OK with me. I was six years away from "The Pension" and had learned to appreciate economy.

I'd learned also to insist on dutch treat years ago. It kept things cleaner somehow; it's surprising how many guys edging into their seventies are still interested in the come-up-to-my-place stuff after they've bought you so much as a hamburger at the Woolco lunch counter. Real elegance. If they only wanted you to sew buttons on a favourite shirt, its last contact with the inside of a washing machine patently long in the past, it was McDonald's they offered.

The spaghetti wasn't too bad, just not very tomato-ey, and I was hungry. At the age of 59 I was belatedly doing my artist-in-a-garret phase and was allowing myself only two meals a day. Not as much for the heady replay of Hemingway *et al.* starving in a Paris attic or its equivalent in some other exotic milieu, but because the roly-poly genes that had come to me undiluted via seven generations of Bavarian peasant women had begun to do their dirty work and I was beginning to huff after the first set of stairs at the Lady Duchess Apartments.

No duchess would have set foot in the place. No charwoman who could afford anything better either. Not Kurt, not me, not Miss Burney, I'm sure – if we had the price of anything better.

"How many times did she bother *you* today?" said Kurt. "This spaghetti is like rubber, even my last wife could do it better, how many times did she bother *you* today?"

"You mean Miss Burney?"

"Of course I mean Miss Burney, weren't you listening at all? Women never listen. I thought you'd be different, but women never listen."

I was beginning to see why the laundry room gossip had Kurt pegged as impossible. He looked gorgeous; he could speak intelligently (and very quickly) on twenty subjects in as many minutes. That he was poor was nothing – we all were in that place. But he had the personality of a nutmeg grater; I'd simply been pretending it didn't bother me.

"I am listening," I said. "The spaghetti tastes pretty good to me."

"I've heard of people whose taste is all in the mouth," said Kurt, "but that opinion certainly could not be levelled at you, my dear, now could it?"

Kurt loved the conundrum of back-handed compliments which, upon consideration, had nothing whatever complimentary about them. Rather than figure this one out I opted for home. I laid my four dollars and a quarter beside his water glass and got up.

"But you haven't had the second helping," said Kurt.

"It was so good I don't need a second go-round," I said. If he got up and followed me I might punch him one in the mouth. As it was, I had decided not to tell him about the red smear of spaghetti sauce that dribbled like Count Dracula's supper at one corner of his mouth. Let someone else tell him. Let Miss Burney tell him when she came for the "twentieth" time in one hour to ask him what time it is. Or to ask where she lived. Or what her name was. Or whatever the hell she supposedly asked Kurt twenty times in any hour of his precious day. Since flinging myself into my garret phase I had trained myself to say *hell* a lot in the inner dialogue.

I huffed up the five flights to my floor, hefted open the stubborn door to the fifth floor hall and thanked my stars my "fully accoutred bachelor suite" was just around the corner. I turned the corner. And there stood this little white-haired biddy with her nose scrunched to the numbers on my door. "Hello," I said.

She turned towards me. "Hello there," she said, stepping towards me and peering. "Who are you then? Do I know you?"

"I'm Vanessa, Miss Burney," I said. "I live here now. I'm new. I'm from Saskatchewan." Who cares?

"Oh yes," she said, "how very nice. Will you tell me, dear, do I live in this place?"

"Yes, Miss Burney. Just down the hall, I believe."

"Not right here? Not behind the numbers on this door?"

"No, Miss Burney. See? There's a name on the mailbox: V. Shaftbury. That's me. Now let's go down the hall and look for *your* name, shall we?"

"Oh yes, dear heavenly father," she said, "let us go like sixty, for I have a pressing call to nature that will not be denied."

She had about her an air that suggested nature had already taken matters into its own hands, but I offered my arm and she groped for any part of me she could clutch and we went like sixty, or at least as fast as her slippery-sloppery orange and purple string slippers would permit.

"Here is your door, Miss Burney," I said. "Shall I help you in?"

She was groping for the whereabouts of the mailbox. She found it and opened it and ran her hand around inside it. "Oh no, dear heavenly father," she said, "no mail again, oh dear, oh dear, oh dearie little me." I tried to open the door to speed things up. It was locked.

"Have you your key then, Miss Burney?" Oh please, dear heavenly father and all the angels, let her have her key.

"Yes, yes, yes," she piped, "we must always carry our key." And she felt about under the grey-white dressing gown, buttoned askew but tightly at the throat, and pulled out a key on a greyed old-fashioned store string. With the forefinger of her left hand she found the key hole and traced its pattern. She bent towards it and with her right hand fitted the key, turned it. "Oh now, dear heavenly father but that's a blessing," she said, "it turns. Did you see that?"

Get in, get in there, 'cause I'm back down that hall like sixty the minute you close the door.

"I said," she said, "'Did you see that?' It tu-u-urns." Not only had it turned, it had released the door. The key was in the door, the string to the key was about Miss Burney's thin little neck. She gave the door a surprising heft with one small orange and purple foot and was drawn into the room along with the swinging door in the manner of a reluctant calf being drawn into the pen on a taut halter rope.

"Oh dear heavenly father," she sang now, "take me home for I have had enough of this durance vile! Please take me home, dear father, for I am weary for you, for you, for you." Her nose was snubbed against the door. I had the devil's own time to disconnect and reconnect all the appropriate items. Then I pointed her towards the bathroom and ran. When I was a kid we used to go to the city sometimes on a Saturday, to the west side market where all the farmers went, and nearby was what everybody called The Comfort Station. Miss Burney's abode had about it something of the do-not-tarry essence of The Comfort Station of long ago.

I hated myself. Or the one of me that still had feelings did. That'll be you someday, you know, that Other One said. You'll wish for someone to lead you home and set you on the pottie and cook a little something for you too, I expect. Who cooks for her? Who does for her?

Aw come on, this is no Dickens storybook, I said, there are government agencies to look after people like that.

Who has told them she even exists? said that Other One. I hate it when She is so logical. It means I won't sleep much that night.

By next morning I had decided I'd call Social Aid. Or some seniors' agency. They must have them here in Manitoba, else what are all those Brits and Swedes studying when they come over? But my phone had been disconnected due to an altercation with ManTel and I was trying to get by without one as long as I could. Social Aid didn't know about it yet and I had better things to do with ten dollars a month. Like springing for an extra jar or two of peanut butter.

There was a dinky little room on the ground floor that was respectfully referred to as the solarium. No sunlight ever reached it, but it was hot as the heart of Old Sol himself all summer. I chugged down the five flights and was just passing the solarium to go out and find a phone when from the dim confines of the room someone called, "Who goes there? Come in here, please. At once, mind you!"

Oh God. In I went. "Good morning, Miss Burney."

"Ah, good morning, my dear. And who might *you* be? I'm afraid I don't see as well as once I used to. It's a dreadful handicap, if I may say so, but one must bear up. Play up, play up, and play the game, am I right? am I right?

"Now. Your name, please."

"It's Vanessa, Miss Burney. Vanessa Shaftbury. *You* know . . . the fifth floor. . ."

"Indeedy do, I most certainly do know the fifth floor, for haven't I lived on it for these thirty-seven years? Oh yes, longer than anyone else in the building. Indeedy do. And you, my dear? You are just moving in? Is someone helping you with the baggage? You mustn't try to carry things up those five flights by yourself; we'll ask Miss Evans when she comes to find you someone to help. She's very good, Miss Evans; she's ever so organized. I admire that in a woman so much, don't you?" Her face seemed animated; her eyes, had there been light enough to check them out, might have been sparkling.

It was like being caught in a time shift. Or at least what I think it must be like to be caught in a time shift. Or an Alfred Hitchcock movie. *This* was the addlepated little old lady who had got her nose snubbed to her own door last night? I was just as glad Miss Burney's eyesight lacked a little something because I'm sure I was gaping like a fish out of water.

Then this very smart young woman came in the door. "Oh my goodness," she said, "let's have a little light on the subject, shall we?" She went about, flicking on lights. I didn't even ask if she was Miss Evans; I turned tail and laboured up the stairs again, swearing if I met Kurt on the way I'd spit in his eye just for the pure hell of it.

There was a note under my door when I got there. It was on pale pink notepaper and had computered hearts spun out all over it. Kurt had brought home my seconds from the spaghetti place and wanted me to come for lunch. He wondered if I could bring half a loaf of buttered bread to eke out the pasta. I tossed the note's pinkness with appropriate disdain into the waste basket.

Then, *Hemingway!* said the Other One into my mind, very, very clearly. I grabbed the pinked hearts up again like sixty and started to plan what to wear.

COCOON

They were wrong. Those poets and philosophers and sayers of wise saws. You *can* go home again. And Adeline had done it. And here she was, comfortable, and safe. And home.

The house was little and it was old. Not European or Mediterranean old, with a history almost as old as the stones in their castles and inns and houses, just old enough to be never really comfort-proof again in thirty below in a Saskatchewan winter, but not old enough to give up on and tear down and start over.

Starting over, in a new, trim, little house with the appropriate R-factored walls and roof and floor would have been, in the long run, more practicable, but it would not have been "coming home".

That meant shunting over corduroyed roads and country trails and bush paths in a second-hand four-wheeled drive 'wagon she hadn't driven since she began having her "troubles" six years ago, finding within herself a surprising amount of raw nerve at the stick shift; that meant skirting thirty-five year old potholes in the farm driveway and drawing up to a small house with its life scars all too apparent: the wrinkly weathered look of cheap paint, some cracked and broken windows, a screen door mended too often and still futile against summer insects – everything wrapped in cobwebs and overgrown with brome grass and nettles and sow thistle and vague memories.

The foundation was firm. No cracks. But at first she hadn't seen that; didn't even think to look. She was two days short of sixty-three; she had been sent here against her will by strident voices-in-the-head that had given her no peace day or night, except in those crazy moments when she was agreeing to come. If she changed her mind they began again: *Go home! Go home! Go home!* She had been to three doctors; she had been to two psychiatrists. And when she could not bear the badgering any longer she quit pacing the floor at four o'clock one morning just as first light was colouring the sky, packed – both methodically and joyfully, as she analyzed it later – and was on her way in two hours' time.

No one in the world knew where she was. Three weeks ago, in one of her "agreeing" times, she had slapped, sight unseen, nearly every penny she had scrambled for for over thirty years into a place she had not seen for forty. The euphoria of owning the place she had lived in as a child lasted for over a week. Then the second-guessing set in. For the first time she knew she was crazy. To let the money go like that, what could she have been thinking of? Well, she hadn't been thinking, that was plain. She could never, never, tell Dr. Watson; he'd have her committed for sure now. And then, of course, the voices came back: *Go home! Go home! Go home!*

Once on the road, they sang. Mostly "going home" songs. How foolish she felt, and how happy. How would she live? What would she do there? She didn't even know yet if the title was clear; didn't know if she really owned it. Yet the voices sang as she drove the familiar roads and read the grid road map once she reached the less-remembered territory; they lapsed into purple silence when she remembered the stale-dated licence plates on the vehicle, took up singing again once she'd rectified the matter, and then delivered harmony until she lurched the 'wagon to a halt in the tangled grass in the middle of the farmyard in deference to the tire traps often hidden in such grass in old places. She got out and was immediately assailed – there was no other word for it – by the perfume of pine resin and of the gum of the Balm of Gilead still guarding the old well-house.

And knew she was home.

Addie awoke the next morning to the chittering of house sparrows and to the realization that, for the first time in over fifty years, she had dreamed about her mother.

It was a shadowy place, that dream place, as if it wore veils. As if the entire dream were wound about with fine filament, with gossamer, perhaps — it was a lovely word, *gossamer*; it was just right for half-hiding things that are best veiled, protected from the knowingness of those who might unravel the threads of a gossamer veil cocooning the most secret heart, the knowingness of those who might then wind their own fine, silver-white, careful spinnings about the laid-bare heart and so keep it safe, safe, within the care of one the heart cannot really belong to — *ought* not belong to, *must* not belong to. For at the heart is where one lies surest, truest, only so long as no one else has access to the patternings that can unravel the threads, disclose the secrets of The One Who Lies Within.

It was as though she was there in the dream twice — or was it as two different Addies? One, on the outside, looking in on the scene through a filmy gossamer; the other a participant inside the dream place.

It was a vast hall of some sort, strung with beads of light beginning in all corners and at the midpoints of the tops and bottoms of the walls, the white beads like drops of dew on a spider's web sprinkle-sparkling in the early morning sun. The vortex of all those beaded strings (or, perhaps, the lair of the spider?) was darkish and so for a few bits of time she did not see her mother. Then she was there. She looked young; forty-ish, maybe. And she did not look like herself at all.

"The least you could do," Addie remembered saying, "if you're going to be in my dream, is to look like yourself!"

Her mother had answered, in characteristic fashion, "Oh, Addie, you silly thing! I can look like whatever I want."

Addie had begun to protest. There ought to be some rules about this. Then her mother had said, her voice quite prim, "You don't own your own dreams, you know; you don't own your own dreams."

Addie thought about that now, snuggling deeper into the cozy double flannel of the sleeping bag tossed late last night upon the unmattressed old brass bed she'd dusted and scrubbed as best she could, given the circumstances. She closed her eyes and wriggled into fetal position; sometimes you could get a dream back that way, if you did it soon enough.

"You don't own your own dreams, you know."

It didn't work this time. Thoughts intruded. This-world thoughts. The cozy bed, first. Then, gratitude, because the house was in much better condition than she'd have dared to hope, had she been in a condition to hope.

Had she been in a condition to hope, to function efficiently enough to hope, she'd have been able to think things out rationally and therefore — it goes without saying — would never have been crazy enough to buy this place in the godforsaken boondocks. This place of peace. The place she had supposed she would never see again.

Grandma's brass bed — the thought brought her circle-around again — the one nobody wanted when it had been offered to the various families when Addie was a child here. When her dad had brought it home he'd stood at the open door propping up the headboard with its two small round globes (St. Paul and St. Luke, to guard the sleeper's sleep, Grandma had often said). "Well, what could I do?" he said. "She seemed to think she was doing us a favour." For two days his smile had been sheepish whenever he looked at Addie's mother.

Who had been in the dream last night. Saying, "You don't own your own dreams, you know."

Maybe we didn't own anything, not even our own minds.

As if in corroboration of this newly-proposed theory there was a sudden flish-flashing of pictures then, the coloured kind, the kind the first psychiatrist had said would disappear if she would take her Vitamin B like a good girl and arrange to visit cancer patients so she could see people worse off than herself.

The pictures were of herself and her cousin Lucy, the bedroom door shut tight, jumping, jumping, jumping, higher and higher, to see who could first touch the ceiling of this very room from this very bed. Lucy, the bold one, the one who had run off to college in Omaha. How many people had ever run off to *college*, for heaven's sake? Leave it to Lucy to make it sound dramatic and daring, and even illicit.

"Broke up the family," she'd written Addie, and truth enough it had, nearly. Now there were the pictures and the sounds and even the smells, somehow, of those recriminating family scenes in which Addie's father was accused of providing the busfare for "the getaway" (He had). The pictures were spinning, spinning. *Steady! Steady on, now!* she told them as she used to when she was a child; it was a trick she had learned in the fields from her father and his horses. When things got too skitterish you told them "*Steady on!*" and they settled down.

Until you had worked for twenty-seven years in the basement of an old government building sorting musty papers and trying to pretend it mattered so that you could bear to pick up your pay cheque at the end of every month.

She hadn't thought of *Steady on!* for years, hadn't had to for all those years in the government basement. Then her job had been phased out, so they said, and *she'd* been phased out too, not at all delicately. And the pictures had started again.

As a child she'd never minded. She'd liked them, in fact. There was no television then, no movies except maybe once a year when *Snow White* came to town, but the mind-movies got in the way later and so she had cured herself of them by looking always beyond them, not permitting them into her line of vision at all.

But in those happy days when she had lived in this house as a child, and had been her father's "hired man" from the age of four, she had learned to stabilize the mind pictures and had supposed everyone else had to do the same — and *did* the same, although it was never taught in school — with some version of the firm yet kindly admonition to go steady on.

The pictures settled down. She wondered if she should get up and take the Vitamin B. She hadn't unpacked much; where in the world would that Vitamin B be? where would be that Vitamin B? would a bee be B enough for a Vitamin B pill? hers were bee-body shape, her body was bee-shaped now in this nice warm sleeping bag, but a bee would be more protein than anything else, those people who ate chocolate ants at parties, those big gross ones (the ants, but sometimes the people too), the big gross ones from Africa, wasn't it Africa? they said it was protein and you got the same only better they said from salt-roasted Saskatchewan grasshoppers, when they got to that part you always got up and went out for air, unless it was winter and then since you had to get bundled up anyway you just went home and found something better to do.

She came to with a start. All that mind-stuff had eliminated the pictures. Just as well. They weren't really good for you. She curled up into an even tighter ball, told the warmth of the sleeping bag how glad she was for it, and speculated about the chances of going back to sleep, never mind relocating elusive dreams.

Her watch had said four-thirty. She hoped that wasn't going to be a pattern . . . oh, yes, patterns, she'd forgotten about patterns, but the bladder had just cut in with the announcement that it was not as pliable as it used to be, something it had been doing for over a year now . . . and always at four-thirty . . . often she'd just managed to get to sleep.

She shuffled about in the eiderdown, leaned out and peered under the bed. Reflex action. Checking under the bed was what your mother often told you to always do if you went visiting on "an overnight".

"Now, before you go to bed, ask Aunt Nettie for the flashlight – she keeps it in the warming oven of the stove to extend the batteries – and go out to the privy just before you go to bed, you'll last longer that way. And before you get into bed check under it to see if she has put a thundermug there for you, she sometimes forgets. If she hasn't, you *ask*, now, mind you! I don't want any reports of bed wetters coming home to me from my dear Sister Nettie, I can tell you that!"

You didn't though. Ask. If the wide china pot with the pale blue flowers wasn't in place you hated to ask, so you told your mind, instead, to wake you up before the bladder got desperate. You didn't know the word *desperate* back then, so you said something that served the purpose. For it always worked.

And you got up always at four-thirty. It would be summertime, but always it was cool at night. You'd tiptoe past your Aunt Nettie's bedroom where Uncle Nils would be snoring deeply. (Come to think of it, maybe it had been Aunt Nettie, who knows? In those days you always blamed the men.)

You'd lift the latch of the porch door slowly, slowly, so it wouldn't creak, and there'd be Old Fred looking up at you from the dew-damp great white stone slab that served as the last step out of (or the first step into) the house of Uncle Nils and Aunt Nettie.

Old Fred never slept, it seemed. He was there every time you came to the door into first dawn light and morning dew, staring.

Old Fred wasn't old. He was the third Old Fred Uncle Nils had had, and was hardly more than a pup, if a St. Bernard can ever be said to be "just" anything. But he was Old Fred anyway, and he didn't like the last Old Fred's doghouse and never had. Aunt Nettie gave him old coats to sleep on then, outside, right near the door, taking away space from the purple pansies she kept in regular rows, year by year, along the front of the house.

But Old Fred preferred the great white stone, and he would follow you then down the path to the privy; you hardly ever cheated and "went" just around the corner of the house. For one thing, that was "low-order habits" and heaven help you if anyone ever found out; for another thing, Old Fred was too fond of investigating bare skin wherever he found it, and if you said "G'wan!" to him when he was lapping your face and ears he went into rearguard action, which was unbearable.

By now Addie's bladder was saying: Hey, you! I mean business! There was no thundermug under the bed, of course. She sighed, wondering briefly if she couldn't *will* one into existence. Fairy godmothers likely used to do so for their charges, but such mundane (or personal) details never made it into the fairy tales along with the golden coach and things like that.

She'd got her feet planted on the pale worn cold linoleum, thankful she'd remembered just before leaving home to stash Mr. Clean under the driver's seat. (Mr. Clean had been sure she'd meant for him to be placed under the driver's *feet*, apparently, for that's where he'd spent most of the journey.) Anyway, the linoleum was now clean, all through the main part of the house.

She'd worn socks to bed, another trick learned early in life, so foot-padding on through to the kitchen and then out to the porch was not too shocking. She slipped into rubber boots – the dew here was always more than generous, it was downright prodigal, to the point of excess. She opened the door and there was a rather vague, filmy Old Fred lying there, staring up at her with those chocolate maplebud eyes. An Old Fred cocooned about with gossamer as the dream had been.

She blinked and he was gone. This house also had for some reason a great white stone slab step. Only bigger. Maybe it was the family version of one-upmanship back then, who knows? The second Old Fred, it used to be said, often mistook the stones, on his nightly rambles about the countryside, and frequently was found on this particular white stone calmly waiting to be told, "Well, come on *in* then, you dear old Fred" or else "Get on home then, you darn old fool", depending on who had found him.

The path to the privy was overgrown, mostly with nettles. She went around the corner of the house, fiddled with clothes, squatted, shivered, said aloud, "I'll wallop any old Fred a good one across the snout if he . . ." and then she saw the truck.

It was in the middle of the yard. Someone was standing beside it, back to her. How long had he been there and was it out of courtesy he was now facing away? She crept around the back and crawled in a window. If she gave no sign, surely he'd go away.

Probably a hunter or a salesman. Maybe the local SaskPower man wanting to sell her a power line. Well, let him cool his heels.

It was very cool in the house. That had been the beauty of this place, her mother had often said. A smallish low house, but one that spread itself out under low-hanging branches of white poplar and hardy spruce; a large slough, mint-edged, a few yards from the lower end of the backyard and garden; a row of shade trees on each of the other two sides of the garden – that seemed to help funnel cool breezes from the water directly to the house. As a result, a wood fire every summer's morning was not just welcome, it was almost mandatory.

Without a fire there would be no tea. Drat! She stole a peek out the window. The truck was still there. It was veiled a bit in the light mist that arose here, most mornings, springtime until freeze-up, because of the nearness of the slough. She could go back to bed and outwait the fellow, but to do without a cup of hot mellow tea was suddenly a physical impossiblity. She lit the fire, shivering, tore off nightclothes and wrestled into dampish overalls and T-shirt, found a sweater and toque to add to the outfit and a second pair of socks to take up the slack in the hiking boots that were to serve her now as field boots *à la* "the good old days".

She was still tying up the boots when there was a tap-tap-tap at the door. "I suppose there's no use to hope it's a woodpecker," she grumbled. She finished tying the boots, sat looking at them until she became itchy-eily with the discomfort of remembrance of standing, herself, on someone's doorstep, knowing they were home, speculating whether it was best to go away or to keep trying lest they weren't really avoiding you but had been in the shower or otherwise indisposed.

"If he's so insensitive – or, heaven forbid, dangerous! – as to call on people at half-past five in the morning, let him stand there," she told the boots, but the body got up and the feet walked her to the door anyway.

Old Fred was there. For sure, this time. And a rather short, smallish – let's say *skinny* – man with sharp features, a prominent Adam's apple, all kinds of hair (once he'd taken off a seemingly brand new John Deere peaked cap it seemed to billow out quickly, giving him a bit of an Einsteinish appearance) and eyes as blue and penetrating as the eyes of the Jesus in the picture with the gold frame on the parlour wall at Grandma Frobisher's a lifetime or so ago.

Surely she'd been standing there with her mouth dropped open for over an hour. She was cold as ice. She must have been standing here agape, keeping him on the great stone step for over an hour, surely.

"Get back to the truck, Apollo," he was saying to Old Fred.

"He's named for a god," she said. "How lovely."

"A space mission," he said. "I heard you were coming. I knew you were here."

"News travels fast," she said.

"*My* way it does," he said, pointing to his head.

"Come in," she said, "the water's on for tea." She didn't know who he was or what he was here for and she certainly didn't care, but she'd just said, "Come on in, the water's on for tea!"

He took off the bright clean white and green John Deere cap, gave the dog a swat with it, said, "Go back to the truck, I said," looked at his cap, seemed to debate a smudge (courtesy, perhaps, of Apollo) brushed it several times across one arm of his denim jacket, seemed satisfied with the result, wiped his feet on the damp stone step and said, "I'll come in now."

"Of course," she said. Of course! She'd been standing planted like a stubborn donkey full in the doorway. A bit of body language? Well, he likely wasn't into reading such. She moved ahead of him into the kitchen. "Come in, yes come in, the water will take a while; I'll hurry it along in a saucepan, shall I?"

"We've got lots of time," he said. He pulled up a chair to the table – why was she so glad she had scrubbed and scoured so late into the night, burning up precious fuel in the camping lantern, hurrying as though it was somehow necessary to have the kitchen and bedroom, at least, as clean as hot water and Mr. Clean and elbow grease could make them before she went to bed?

"Smoke?" he said. She shook her head. "OK?" he asked, tapping a bluish pack of some kind of smoking tobacco at his own chest.

She hated cigarette smoke. She nodded. "I think I saw an old sardine can somewhere about, yesterday; it can do you for an ash tray."

"It's OK, I carry my own." He swung one leg over the knee of the other and indicated his pants cuff. "My dad taught us that." He was already rolling a smoke. "You don't know me, I bet." She hoped he wasn't the kind who tried to make you guess; she hated that. "I'm a Crowther. Daniel Crowther. Danny. You were my teacher."

"I *couldn't* have been." Some grain of good sense was telling her it was time to add wood to the fire, get out the tea things: they're in the Co-op creamed corn box, remember, the cupboards haven't been scrubbed yet. "I only taught one year," she said. "I wasn't very good. It was a painful experience. I left."

"I remember." Silence. Just *what* did he remember? "You were the best they'd ever had here. Even Mr. Henderson said so."

"*Henderson*? . . . oh my, yes: Jerome K. Mr. Wonderful Henderson. Chairman of the school board, Member of Session in the church, *he's* the one who . . ." He's the one who promised you the moon; lying under the great spruce in the middle of the schoolyard on the scarlet red robe from the back seat of his Model A he promised you the moon and stars and you believed every word of it; two weeks later he introduced you to his "intended" at a school dance.

"I never taught again," she said. "I went down to Regina and got a job. Government." That used to be a thing around here, a government job. You never had to uphold the family honour any further once you'd reported a ne'er-do-well (or a fallen daughter) had "gone on down to Regina and got himself (herself) a government job".

"I know," he said.

What in hell *did* he know? Then all at once it was decided: there was no point whatsoever in having the mind engaged here. What was there, after all these years, to protect? to deny? And who was this bloke so that it even mattered? "Just who in hell are you?" she said. She had the heavy saucepan in one hand to pour wildly boiling water onto the leaves in the smaller pan that was to serve as teapot.

"I'm a Crowther. Daniel. Danny, you called me. I've already said."

She made the tea, set out the one cup and saucer for him, the top of the thermos flask for herself, sat down across from him, within arm's reach of the brewing tea set aside on the stove's reservoir. She looked him full in the face, taking the time to do it. There were no inner pictures to help her. "I'm really sorry," she said. "I have forgotten. I don't recognize you . . . any family resemblance, that sort of thing . . ."

"There *is* no family resemblance. If you're looking for my dad. He wasn't really my dad. Mother worked for somebody who wouldn't honour her, after. He went back to England and brought himself back a real wife. Everybody knew."

"I didn't."

"I guess your folks didn't talk over such things much. Then she — I wasn't quite born yet — came to look after Dad and his family. Then they got married. After Meredith was on the way. You remember Meredith?"

"Sorry."

"Meredith was the smart one. I'm the one was in Grade Three for too many years. When you came I couldn't read. You helped me a lot. You got me into Grade Four, Mother said it was a miracle. She's gone now. She never forgot you though. Me either. I'll never forget." He got up and walked the stub end of his cigarette to the stove, lifted a lid over the fire-box and dropped it in. "Hard on the pants cuff, that." He grinned. He had nice teeth. "You get to be kind of careful about that when you have to mend 'em yourself."

He drank his tea standing up, on the move. He'd come prepared to fix and mend. He'd been keeping an eye on the place ever since the Dambowskis left. They were good people, good workers; they made their living for years off this one quarter, just like people in the old days did: cows, pigs, chickens, garden truck, whatever it took.

Had they asked him to look after it?

"No, I just knew *you* were coming back."

He'd meant to mend the windows and screens earlier, but he was looking after Mr. Henderson's place too. That's where he lived, on Mr. Henderson's place. Since the Hendersons moved, retired into town, he'd been living in the house; before that he'd fixed up a place for himself in the hayloft, it was pretty nice there, smelled of fresh hay all year 'round, even after the loft hadn't seen hay for five years.

He'd never made it past Grade Four, see? He'd just stayed home and worked on the farm until his folks quit and sold to Meredith.

It wasn't he and Meredith didn't see eye to eye, Meredith had said. They didn't, but Meredith had said, "It isn't we don't see eye to eye, Daniel, but if you live here you can't get Welfare, see what I mean?" Meredith knew about these things. Meredith had said, "I can keep you busy here on the home place, that's for sure, but if you live here you can't get Welfare, see? And I sure can't afford to keep you and that's a fact."

He'd walked to Mr. Henderson's that same night. In the dark. He didn't have a truck then, not even a bike. He'd walked the ten miles and Mr. Henderson said Sure, he could sure use a hand. And that's where he was yet. He looked after things – the house, the outbuildings, the fences and corrals. The land was rented out. Meredith had tried to get it but wouldn't come to Mr. Henderson's terms. And now Daniel looked after things and paid the power and phone and things out of his Welfare and sawed Mr. Henderson twenty cords of wood a winter for his place in town since coal and oil cost money.

He'd started looking after things here too, after the Dambowskis left, only things had kind of got ahead of him the year he got sick and kept seeing St. Francis and his birds. (Some of them had red and yellow heads, redder than any red you'd ever see on this earth, and the yellow was the yellow of buttercups in a green meadow when the sun is just right in the sky to make them realer than real.) That was the year he kept hearing the music of the spheres too, in the bush when he was cutting wood.

She speculated then about telling him about the voices. The ones she hadn't heard since she'd hit the road to come here. Then, *Shut up!* said someone inside the head, very, very clearly. So, "I think it's time to eat," she said. "Do you realize it's two o'clock?"

"Time goes when you're having fun," he said.

Lunch, which was really breakfast, consisted of tinned ham and powdered eggs, fresh tomatoes, and lots of bread and coffee. Daniel dropped his tools on command and lit a cigarette. "You should eat first," she said. Oh, stupid! Whose business was it anyway?

"Why?"

"It will spoil your appetite."

"Wait and see."

It hadn't. After they had eaten she set the dishes to soak in a pan of water at the back of the stove and they walked down to the slough where ducks – mallards and pintails and dark homely shovellers – were having a merry time of it splashing and visiting and squabbling. The perfume of wolf willow was light upon the air and a redwing blackbird sang courteous defence of its territory from atop a cattail swaying in the slight breeze. The sun was golden; it wrapped the body in a toasty warmth you could almost see; as they sauntered along Addie began to think she heard the humming of bees about her head. She stopped, looked, listened again.

"What?" he said.

"Nothing."

They started up a fox. After scrambling away for a bit, it turned and looked back over its shoulder at them, squatting as a cat does, on its haunches, not adopting the rooted, stockstill, over-the-shoulder stance a dog or coyote uses when it means to inspect.

Neither of them said much. Having someone *around* you, warm and silent, is quite different from having someone with you, Addie decided. It was like the times with the first psychiatrist, the one who gave her away – his words – to a buddy because, he said (quite rightly), she had begun to care for him in a way that made a professional relationship "untenable". She had forgotten his name by now; there must be a reason for that.

At the slough's edge they sat for a while in the sun. About the time she began thinking about the mosquitoes she'd have to contend with that night because of the unscreened windows, he said, "Time to finish those windows if we head back now; you don't want them dancing on your nose again tonight."

After a late supper they sat on the steps in the dusk and watched the deer come up through the yard, picking their way with that delicate elegance deer have – pick, pick, picking their little feet along the ground; pick, pick, picking a bite here, a morsel there.

"You'll have good meat this winter," he said. His voice was very quiet. He didn't whisper, because of the deer, his voice simply melded into the night's temperate sounds — the crickets in the nettles, the frogs in the slough, a nighthawk demonstrating its intentions high overhead. At first she was sure she hadn't heard him right.

"Good meat," he said again, waving a lit cigarette towards the deer.

"My goodness, I couldn't! They're too beautiful!"

"Wait till they've clipped your garden to the bare dirt a few times," he said, "or you've been living on canned Spam for half the winter." He butted his cigarette, tongue-clicked Apollo/Old Fred into being, and made off with a brief wave of the hand.

Addie went inside right away. It wasn't that she was tired; she wasn't. She never really ever got tired any more, that was part of her trouble, part of the restlessness, the doctors had said. They all had given her sleeping pills, but for some reason she could never make herself take them. Rather, she lay awake, sometimes most of the night, watching the blue and white lights that hovered around her in the darkened bedroom, listening, almost appreciatively, to the faint electrical hum that surrounded her head like a bee swarm as soon as she shut out the sounds of the world from the quiet, dark silence of that little room.

Eventually, those almost sleepless nights, she would slip away into dreams, dreams, dreams, some of them horrendous, some so full of colour and sound and light it was impossible to find the words to describe them. She would be awake again too early, unable to get back to sleep and with the same restlessness stirring in her, so that she would have to get up and consider another day in which there was nothing she wanted and no one she cared to be with.

Now, alone again in the little farmhouse, she built a low fire in the tiny heater near the bedroom, washed as best she could in a tin basin with tepid water from the kitchen stove's copper reservoir, wormed into the sleeping bag atop the bed springs of the old brass bed.

Daniel had eyed "such a set-up" with a shaking of his head. "There's a spare bedroom at Mr. Henderson's place," he said.

"*No thank you!*" She had turned on her heel and stamped away.

"He talks about you," he had called after her. "Whenever he comes he talks about you."

Briefly, anger flared again now as the mind replayed the scene. But the blue and white stars of night came soon into the cozy darkness of the room; they were larger here and brighter than they had been in the city. Through them she watched the flames rise and fall, rise and fall, behind the cracked isinglass windows in the little heater. She had added a little too much wood. She hoped the Dambowskis had believed in cleaning stove pipes and chimneys. Then she was out like a light.

In the morning she was up before the sun, chopping wood. The house held the damp morning chill that used to give her delightful shivers as a child and send her scurrying to dress near the stove already alive and harbouring the aromas of fresh coffee and of brown grainy porridge cooking with soft plp-plp-plops at the back of the stove.

The axe hadn't been sharpened since her last camping effort too many years ago, but she made do with slim deadfalls that could be whacked into firebox length if you put enough muscle to it. I hope I'll see this Daniel again soon and that he has access to a chain saw, she told herself, puffing, taking another good crack with the axe.

Once fortified with bread and jam and coffee – the margarine was down the well in an old metal pail dangling from a sound chain spiked to less secure cribbing, and she couldn't face discovering chain and bucket, plus polyunsaturated, had sunk into the deep, never to be seen again – she made a foray into the yard.

In the log outbuilding that had once been her father's tool shed – and Mr. Dambowski's too, from the look of things – she found a scythe so dusty and cobwebbed it seemed to have been largely protected from rust. Clustered on the rafter above it, at the very tip of the rusty blade, grew a veritable village of grey-white cocoons. She wondered if they had held – perhaps still held – the pupae of "pumpkin pie" butterflies, those lovely orange and black and white winged ones that used to flitter about everywhere you went as a child on this peaceful and protected land.

There must be some reason Mr. Dambowski had left the scythe behind. She lifted it carefully from its place: there you go, the blade wobbled like crazy and, upon inspection, it was fair dull. Great, something else to be sharpened if she ever came across a whetstone – and could manage the knack of it. In the meantime, it might at least bend (if not bow) the backs of the nettles and brome grass on the Road to Mandalay. She had forgotten all about that Road to Mandalay thing, one of the euphemisms her father had employed when speaking to females about such "delicate" matters as excretion.

The scythe was light, thank heaven. And did the job surprisingly well. She eventually got into the rhythm of it and it felt good – good to the muscles and good to the eyes as the weeds and grass fell in sweep after even sweep before her.

I used to be good at this, she told her mind. When she had cleared the path and territory around the privy she celebrated by sweeping out the accumulated sand and cobwebs and dust, using the broom Mrs. Dambowski had left installed, one might presume, for the purpose, then giving it the Mr. Clean treatment by sloshing hot water plus disinfectant all over, as high and as wide as it would go, then sweeping, sweeping until all was clean and ready for duty.

By mid-afternoon she was tired. For the first time in years she was tired. But there was still a section of the front yard, within the house fence, that needed action and she was loath to quit. She was scything away quite happily, albeit quite spasmodically, and sweating profusely, when she heard the sound of a truck working its way up the stony, chewed-up lane. One could never see who was coming up into the yard until they were actually there. Her mother had often complained of it; she said you never knew whether you ought to be changing into a clean apron until people were at the front garden gate.

In this case it was, of course, Daniel. And Apollo. Who kept threatening to knock down the slight frame of his good buddy through half-hearted attempts at snatching away the box Daniel was carrying.

In it were milk and butter and bread and four fresh deer steaks, thick-cut. "The rest of the meat is in the ice house. I have . . . Mr. Henderson's place has an ice house," he said.

She looked at that meat and saw deer grazing in the front yard, *her* deer, *her* front yard. She nearly gagged. She knew she couldn't eat it, wouldn't eat it, but by the time Daniel had served it up, fried, with onions browned in the buttered dripping, she ate all he had put on her plate.

Daniel kept a cow. Daniel baked his own bread. Daniel not only had a chain saw, he had it with him. Daniel read minds, perhaps?

That evening, sitting on the steps again, watching the deer again, replete with a second round of venison, coffee and bread, she tackled him.

"Every time I think of something to be done you stop what you're doing and offer to do what is in my mind. Every time I think of someone from the old days, in less than a minute you are telling me a story about them. When my thoughts went back to the city for a while you immediately began to tell me about how it felt when Meredith told you . . . asked you . . . when you had to leave your home. Are you reading my mind, Daniel?"

"Maybe I am reading *you,*" he said. "What does it matter? Things are getting done."

"About that . . .I want to pay you."

"No."

"But . . ."

"No. I said no."

They sat in silence then. He smoked another cigarette, worked the butt into the moist earth with the toe of one boot. Then he got up and whistled up Apollo. As they walked towards the truck the deer, as one, raised their heads from grazing, stood still as stone while the buck blew noisily in and out to take the scent. Then, as if on cue, they took off, white flags flying, to sail over the barbed-wire fence and melt into the bush.

With the flash of a hand, almost, Daniel too was gone.

He did not return for a week. By the end of the second day she was berating herself. Alternately she waged the war of "I should have *made* him take the money" against "Why in heaven's name did I offer him money, people around here don't do things that way".

In the meantime she worked hard. It was a pleasure. One day she drove into town, having become at one and the same time both appalled at the length of the Things Needed list and sharply aware that the Things Needing Doing list could not be proceeded with unless the materials and tools somehow presented themselves on the scene. In town an old man stopped her to say she looked like her mother; at the hardware they recognized the name, took her to coffee, talked for over an hour.

When Daniel came back everything was just the same, as casual as ever. "What's for today then?"

"I hate to tell you."

"I won't die."

She passed him the list of things that needed repair. "What's this then?"

"It's all the things to do you just said you won't die from. 'I won't die', you said; I heard you. Here; read 'em and weep."

"*You* read them to me one by one and one by one they'll get done."

So that was the way *that* was going to be. She nodded.

There was an auction sale this Saturday, did she want to go? Yes. There was a picture show in town tomorrow, did she want to go? Yes. That night, as he was leaving, she walked to the truck with him. With Apollo settled in on the passenger seat he leaned out the window to flash his one-handed good-night. She leaned over and kissed him. "You taste of wolf willow. And of tobacco," she said.

Then it was two weeks later. They were sitting on the steps at dusk, watching the deer.

"You're not smoking," she said.

"Don't seem to want it."

"Your mouth tastes better now, I'll bet." Oh, for heaven sake! he'll think that's a come-on. Well, *is* it?

"I'll be fifty tomorrow."

Relief. "Good. I'll bake you a cake. I'm really getting to know that oven."

"You've got it beat. I've noticed."

Silence. Across the slough a coyote howled. It was a long, drawn-out protest. In spite of herself, she shivered. Foxes she liked, they were silent. Coyotes ought never to have learned how to cry.

When this one had lapsed into silence Daniel said, "Mr. Henderson was down."

Silence.

"He asked about you."

Silence.

"His wife died last year."

Silence. Long-lasting. Then she said, "It was too long ago."

"He wants to see you."

She did not hesitate. "No."

Silence. The coyote again.

He turned to her. "I could stay the night," he said. "If it would help."

"Yes," she said. "We'll go in soon. Let's watch the deer yet awhile."

He got up, took off his shirt and placed it about her shoulders. When he sat down again he sat closer to her.

They sat in silence and watched the deer.

WANTED

"I'm Billy the Kid," he said.

"Mm," I said. I had been with this guy for less than three days and he was wearing thin, to say the least of it. We'd met in Honolulu, in a little park-ish green patch away from the touristy stuff. I was just sitting in the sun and watching: People. Pigeons. A funny plump little bird with a red, red top-knot, a bit cocky. Sometime later I found out its name but forgot it again; it didn't seem to matter enough to try to remember.

I'm like that. At first, when there's something I don't know, I can't stand it, I have to find out. As soon as I do, the information, fascinating or dull as dish-water – as my mother's old auntie used to say – all drifts away and I'm back to square one, ignorant. But, somehow, satisfied.

I was fifty-two years old. He was sixty-five. I remember *that,* all right. When you are "approaching your gold and silver years", as the insurance ads say, and living alone besides, your mind has got itself set for finding out the two essentials (well, let's say two of the *three* essentials) about a man within three minutes of meeting him.

It's not so hard. Even if he's alone, never assume. After the first How are you's, pretty soon it's "And how is *your wife* enjoying Honolulu?" See? Just a little emphasis on the crucial item to make sure he doesn't ignore it.

If he says he hasn't got one – if he's even fair in the looks department, you should be so lucky – you soon find a time to say something along the lines of, "You look so young! I guess you weren't in the War by any chance, were you?"

They love to tell you about the war; I mean, who's going to check records or anything?

The War, to any Canadian over the age of fifty, means the second big one, Churchill's and Hitler's. If they ask, "Which war?" you know you're barking up the wrong tree: they're either too young or too old or too grassy green like the old song had it back in your salad days when there were no men around either because they'd all gone to the war. If you're from North Battleford, Saskatchewan and single – well, most of the time – you've already found out years ago there are no men left around because they're either good and married, or else they've died off being very good to their wives: going out to start the car at thirty-five below while The Wife waits inside in the warm; shovelling six-foot snowdrifts before going to work at the mine because The Wife ain't supposed to and a six-foot son is too busy studying for university or has told you to go to hell over it twice already. When you work at the same truck-stop café for twenty-seven years you hear a lot – a lot more than you want to, to tell the truth of it.

So when I met this Billy the Kid guy in Honolulu, I was pretty impressed. He had no wife and no kids and he looked a lot younger than what he laid claim to. He was from Truth or Consequences, New Mexico. Honest, Truth or Consequences! I laughed right out loud when he said it. He was a short, beefy ex-cop; his hair was still as red as red can be, maybe he doctored it up a little, but who cares, it looked good on him, and he had plenty of it. When he'd been a cop he was in Chicago, but that doesn't matter; it's just if you ever get to little old Truth or Consequences, New Mexico you'll see there's no need for a cop and not even any place to put him.

Anyway, this guy was heavy-set for all there was to him, but he wasn't really jowly yet, and his bright red Hawaiian shirt with hula ladies all over it fit not too snug over the beginnings of a beer belly – or donut belly, as we used to say at the Four Star Truck Stop. He was dressed to the nines – in a touristy way, true enough – and pretty sharp.

We hardly had time for more than the preliminaries. The guy I'd gone to Hawaii with came back too soon. He had a broken marriage, a sullen sixty-seven years under his belt, and a bad bladder. He didn't qualify in the third essential department so at least we had separate beds. We were travelling as "good buddies", a pretty modern thing for him to do, he kept telling me.

He was still "in sales" back home and wherever he went he kept running after prospects (or what he saw as prospects), so he'd followed some Toronto business "tycoon" into the Honolulu main post office with orders for me to just cool my heels for a while.

I went looking for a park bench – I was wearing heels, of all the dumb things – and in the heat they were murder. I found the bench and on one end of it this red-headed Alphonse Joseph McCarthy. He was the only Alphonse I'd ever met. I suppose there might have been others, but who in his right mind would introduce himself as Alphonse if he could get by with Al? But then again, maybe that's what it means to be a beefy ex-cop from Chicago. You know what they say about Chicago.

Anyway, this guy was good looking in a homely kind of Spencer Tracy way, the ears and all, and something told me he was likely still equipped with the third essential (which, to tell the truth of it, hadn't been too essential to me for a few years already by then, but it never paid to admit it to those younger truckers who came along, at loose ends – it generally meant between marriages – and looking for a shoulder to cry on).

So, as I say, this new guy and I didn't have a whole lot of time alone, but he said he liked to get away to the ocean during the hottest months in New Mexico. Not that he didn't have an air-conditioned house. He did. And a blind old dog he hated to put in a kennel. And he was always on the look-out for Canadians (he trusted Canadians, he liked them, he said) to come and live in his place and look after the dog. No rent. Air-conditioning, remember. Just phone and come.

Well, eventually I did. The good buddy system hadn't worked out too well and I was soon on my own again. When you've run a busy café as long as I have and kept six people dancing to your tune (I mean, no dishtowels slung over the shoulder, no gum chewing or runs in the nylons, *clean* uniforms always, and I mean forget the jeans and tight T-shirts, this is a place to *eat*, remember) after a lot of years running somebody else's show in a way that got you automatic raises every first of January and a lot of "Hey, you're too young to talk retirement, Rose, you stick with us for a few years yet" from the bosses, why, you don't take to cooling your heels much while your good buddy runs chasing a hopeful twenty gross of plastic doggie doo, or whatever, three times during a dinner date.

But anyway, time slips away on you and you're thinking retirement whether you talk about it or not. And when you're shovelling your car out of the driveway for the third time in one December week in jolly old North Battleford, Saskatchewan, you keep thinking about that little place the red-headed Yankee has in laughable Truth or Consequences in lovely warm New Mexico, and you're pretty sure you'd be happy there with*out* air-conditioning; in fact, you're pretty sure you'd be glad to turn a heater on down there even in July.

It takes more years than it should have, but you do it. You make the phone call and he's still at that number and "ver-*ry* interested" in letting you have his place, come down as soon as you can and look it over. The way things go, the snow is gone by the time you connect with a seat sale and go.

Alphonse Joseph is supposed to meet you at the airport in Albuquerque; you're looking for him all over the place, saying to yourself, The bugger's let me down after all, when this real lardy (and I mean *lardy*) guy with three chins and a belly that puts Beer Keg Kelly, who drives for Star Lines out of Saskatoon, to sure and all shame, is pushing people aside out of the road left, right and straight ahead of him. On his way to me. He's wearing the red Hawaiian shirt over a not-so-white T-shirt and no chance in this world he'd get done up even the top button let alone the ones around his ample middle. He's wearing a ten-gallon stetson and it's seen better days. To put it politely.

Next thing he's got me in a bear hug and he's kissing me. Right on the lips. Big wet stuff. The kind you wouldn't put up with from a regular. He doesn't take off his hat to do it.

Well, OK. He drives a Lincoln Continental. Not so white. It's big and it's fast and it's noisy. I have a sister who is a school teacher and who says everything sharp and to the point. When this guy and I were barrelling down the road to Truth and Consequences – OK, Truth *or* Consequences – with the Lincoln laying a blue trail of exhaust behind us and Alphonse Joseph bluing up the car with a black Corona as thick as a big man's thumb, I heard, as clear as clear, my sister say: En-*tire*-ly appropriate, wait and see!

Within twenty minutes I'd already learned more than I wanted to handle: (1) it is hotter than hell in New Mexico when you have arrived dressed as a lady; (2) Truth or Consequences, New Mexico, is, you bet your belly band, young lady, named after the radio show of over thirty years ago, sure you remember that; in fact, the town deliberately, you bet, changed its name from Hot Springs, which was a pretty drab name, you have to admit (In the back of my head somewhere there was my sister saying: *Typ*-ical southern entrepreneurship, you'll soon have a belly band full of it, Sis, wait and see!);

(3) Alphonse Joseph – Call me A.J., young lady! – is *not* on his way to ocean tides for the summer, he is staying put to get to know me better.

I wouldn't live in a place like his for all the tea in China. In fact, for all the old emperors' palaces, the whole batch. He had more stuff crammed into that little place than old Henrietta Salisbury who used to walk the streets of Winnipeg for years picking up this, that, and everything inbetween so that when she died – my mother was one of the church ladies who went in and tried to clean the place out – they found it crammed to the gills with everything you can imagine from empty egg cartons and great balls made of the tinfoil box liners from cigarette packages, to garden gates and half an old-fashioned buggy for which she seemed to have been sewing a black velveteen seat cover embroidered with the glass beads from worn-out moccasins.

I was set to do the cooking. You can bet your belly band Alphonse Joseph McCarthy would not insult a lady who was a chef by profession by taking her out to supper in a poor little watering hole like T or C, New Mexico. He'd bought good steaks, though, and they were waiting for me in the fridge. I had to fight my way to them though through a thick green generalized fuzziness that turned out to be things left too long "in the tepid confines" as my sister would say, of a fridge set permanently at Economy.

To set the table I sort of just shoved aside the papers and pill bottles and old socks and the two pistols – going pretty gingerly with the pistols: one was a big brute that he called his "favourite six-shooter", which left the door open for there being others somewhere about); the other was a really small thing, kind of cute, in a way. I shoved everything as far as I could to one end of the long table – making sure the dead socks fell off, accidentally on purpose – ready to set out the plates and cutlery.

I boiled a whole lot of water. Canadians like lots of tea, I told A.J. He said, "I thought that was the goddam Limeys," and I said, "Well, the rest of us too." Then, while he was outside calling in the blind dog to share the steaks with us, I quickly dumped a bunch of dishes in the sink and poured boiling water over everything. That kind of re-shaped a couple of plastic things but I shoved them into a drawer, well to the back, and figured I'd handle that little *faux pas* somewhere down the road if I had to.

My supper was mostly tea. A.J. "put a little fire under the belly band" with as much Southern Comfort as the tea in his cup left room for. From the second cup on he waved away the tea.

By ten-thirty we had covered his family tree "in the auld land" and in Chicago; we'd wallowed through his three marriages, the last one to " a little screw-happy Filipino who got into this Woman's Lib thing as soon as I'd got her a job at City Hall; typical: do 'em a favour and next thing they're yelling they've got rights, too, we should leave 'em all where they belong, so I kicked her out and that was that".

That *wasn't* that, so far as the evening went. I was desperate for sleep, to say nothing of some Canadian-type air-conditioning, the local version seeming to consist of a small fan and an open door. New Mexico is *not* flyless, no matter what anybody tries to tell you. At least where your host keeps a poor big old tired dumb Airedale with lots of hair, leaky ears, and not one snitch of modesty about his bathroom habits. Oh yes, and thirty pigeons. A.J. had clean forgotten to mention the thirty pigeons. Of which there would have been three thousand, by now, you can bet your belly band, only he stole the eggs every morning from the nests and pitched them out. (Some had landed on the dog – a good long while ago – I'm pretty sure of that.)

"Remember now, Rose," my sister had said, after her final tsk-tsk-tsking about this trip, "it's sound policy to make firm mention of one's need for sleep the first night after a plane trip." What with the long day and peculiar events, to say nothing of the cigar smoke, I'd gone into the kind of never-never land in which you get those instant replays of good advice you had thought you were turning a deaf ear to. We were sitting on the front room couch by now. It was pretty lumpy and A.J. was sitting too close.

"I hate to be a party-pooper," I said, at close to midnight, "but back home I'd be sound asleep by now." By then I'd heard all about the Dagos who ran Chicago, about the Jews who ran the banks and wouldn't give him a loan when his mother was dying. But Alphonse just poured another shot of Southern Comfort and launched into Vietnam and Cambodia and "gutless presidents who listen to bleeding-heart liberals instead of pouring on all the coals when they've got enough nice little nukies to blow up the whole world, never mind some little piss-pot country that means nothing to nobody."

All the while he talked he played with one of the pistols from the kitchen table.

"Excuse me," I said once, "but is that thing loaded?"

"Never tell your secrets to a woman," he said, and winked. He put the barrel in his mouth and pulled the trigger and, God help me, I caught myself thinking, I guess I can stand the blood.

"That's how we scared the bastards," he said. And we were into a blow-by-blow of his public service as a loo-tenant in the Chicago police. My eyes glazed over, I'm sure, and I turned off his voice as best I could while trying to do the same for the ripe smell of eggy dog, seeing that Old Prince seemed to have grown very fond of me. He'd squirrelled his way between A.J. and me on the couch – a mixed blessing.

"It's your poor-fume," allowed A.J.

"I never wear any," I said.

"It's the poor-fume of *woman*!" he roared. "Old Prince just loves it. Me too. The hotter the day the higher the poor-fume, you can bet your belly band on that." He winked again. The Harlequins would say he winked broadly. (En-*tire*-ly appropriate, under the circs; wait and see! My sister, the school teacher. Who seems to come through loud and clear when you're tireder than you've ever been after a twelve-hour shift at the Truck Stop on a hot day in July and somebody keeps talking your ear off about stuff you do not want to know.)

Being a cop even in North Battleford, Saskatchewan I don't want to know about. Truckers, in a way, are bad enough. I have to feed them and look after them and they're a great bunch in their own way, but there's lots I don't want to know. About how you make a thirty-six-hour run in thirty and get away with it. About picking up "nice stuff" on the road. Sometimes the "stuff" means long hair and legs and tight jeans, see? and I don't want to hear it – I have young nieces who think they should do the sixties thing and they're always talking about hitchhiking around the world.

For sure and all I did not want to hear how this short fat guy knocking back Comfort had "taken care of" his small territory in dirty big Chicago, and I shut it out as best I could. But then, " . . . goddam liberals," he was bellering, "you have to teach 'em! Canadians aren't like that. I've met 'em in Hawaii and Mexico and in Alaska and they're not like that; they *respect* a cop; but these lousy liberals, you can thank God you don't seem to have 'em in Canada, we picked one of 'em up one night . . . on one of them protest marches . . . We didn't *have* to rough him up, I guess, but you know how these smart-ass university types are – know everything, always demanding rights. Rights for *everybody*. So I says to him,

'How'd you like to spend a night in jail with one o' them?' Know what he said? He said, 'All men are my brothers.' That's what he said.

"So I says to my flunkie, 'Now you make good and sure you dump him in with the biggest, blackest, ugliest nigger you can find; one that *likes* white men, *you* know what I mean.'"

I remember now as clear as anything how my body jolted itself upright on that lumpy couch. As if it had a mind of its own. My feet slid into take-off position. Mouth fell open. I could smell something worse than dirty dog in that room, I don't know to this day what it was, and even the tea supper seemed to want to surface just then.

Shut your trap and keep still! That was not Dear Sis reporting in. Inside my head, though, somebody – a man, I think – was giving hard advice.

"Next morning he was blubbering. And begging for a doctor," said A.J., scratching Old Prince behind one ear. "Poor old fella," he said, "poor old fella." He drained his teacup. "One less liberal went home that day, you can bet your belly band, young lady; let's go to bed."

It turned out there was one bedroom and one bed. He had a "terrible bad back" and couldn't sleep on a couch, he said, but he was sure we'd get along fine, just fine, he felt like a young buck having such a handsome young lady in the house.

Desperation. I can't remember exactly what I said. At first something about Aids, I think. When in doubt, go for broke. "I'll take my chances on a nice clean little Canadian filly," he said. "I like Canadians; you can trust 'em." I invented bleeding next. It started on the plane, I'd have to get back home right away and get it checked out; it could be cancer, one never knew about these things, just better head for home where doctors were cheaper. Sorry.

He looked me up and down and never said a word. "I'll take the couch," I said, but he grabbed up a grey old thing off the bed (I figured out later it was a girdle for his bad back. And then, like a stupe, I was sorry I hadn't *insisted* on the couch). Then he stumbled around collecting some other things, including a pair of hand flexers from under the bed and a chunk of partly-eaten dog biscuit. Then he growled out.

Next morning I had a show of blood! I darn near died right there on the spot. Then I settled down and decided, if it *is* cancer I guess it's been around for a while; and I feel pretty good so I'm going to pretend it isn't there until I get home and then I'll deal with it. So I sneaked out the door and went for a walk.

That early in the morning New Mexico is glorious. I went looking for a phone to call the airport (I didn't dare to do it from the cop's house). It would cost two hundred bucks extra to go home early but all I said was "How soon?" and had to hold on tight when they said not till tomorrow. Then I walked. And walked. There was good green grass and the smell of roses and something that might have been honeysuckle, though that wasn't too likely. The sky was as blue as a Saskatchewan sky and the air as sweet as the air of the lake country back home.

The people I met were nice. Very nice. Polite and friendly. They liked Canadians, they kept saying. "I like you too," I said. The sun was . . . well, at the risk of sounding religious, which I definitely am not, (I'm not even like these new psychics and whatever, like my sister) but at the risk of sounding churchy I somehow have to say the sun was a blessing. It blessed the day – and me, too, it seemed to me. It wasn't hot sand and desert, it was nice, very nice.

Until about ten o'clock. Then things began to fry, so I headed back.

A.J. and Old Prince hadn't waited for me to "do" breakfast for them, thank the Lord. They'd already put a panful of sausage and eggs under the belly band and were busily throwing (or avoiding, as the case may be) eggs from the pigeon nests.

"We'll take the homers for a fly today," said A.J., "as soon as you get a little something under your belly band, young lady." He seemed harmless as all get-out. I wondered if last night had been all a dream – I'm not used to flying – and I kind of wished I hadn't changed my plane flight.

We headed for "hill country". It was cooler up there, and as pretty as can be. We soon let the birds go. It was kind of neat, seeing them circle and circle, with a lot of flash-flashing of silver-white in the sun, then settle into a sure weaving of the canyon towards home.

"They'll be home long before we get to Fort Sumner," said A.J. "I love them birds. Love how they fly, you know that?"

It was kind of nice then, for quite a while. The miles flew. I guess we pretty well did too, at plus or minus eighty miles the hour. I'd rounded up lots to eat and drink for the long haul and when I parcelled anything out to him he took it as grateful as a kid, almost, and seemed content.

After being fed he went into a kind of dreamy state. The Lincoln was at home in the carport. He was driving a beat-up Ford half-ton because it was set up for carrying the birds.

After a while, cruising nice and easy away from the main highway along a smooth road with hardly any traffic on it, he got to talking about what it was like there in the old days, back when the West was being tamed and settled. The Pecos River came into it, and Kit Carson and a bunch of Navajos and a Reserve that hadn't worked out around this Fort Sumner we were going to see. And also into it came Sheriff Pat Garrett and this Billy the Kid.

I used to think Billy the Kid was something made up for the movies or for a comic book, but I didn't say so. We pulled into a parking lot. Beside some sort of touristy Wild West log building. A stockade all around, at the back. A sign: THIS WAY TO BILLY THE KID GRAVE.

"I'm Billy the Kid," he said, A.J. said.

"Mm," I said.

We sat there, in the cab of the half-ton, saying nothing. We sat there for what seemed a long time. I was about to say, "Shall we go in? I'll be glad to pay," when: *Shut your trap!* said that man's voice from somewhere in the back of the head.

"I'm Billy the Kid." He was at it again. He was staring straight ahead.

"Uh . . . right!" I said. It does not pay to even breathe too hard when peculiar things happen so far from home.

"I'm glad you came," he said. "This is my place. My story is here. My energies are here. I'm not what is said in there. In the newspapers, in the words they keep alive. I am . . . was . . . *am* better than that. Kinder. You are one who can help things. He will not go in with you; he cannot bear it; do not ask."

A.J. turned suddenly towards me. No, it was more as if something jerked him around to face me. "This is a place I come to, lots," he said. "Billy the Kid is my all-time hero. Always was. Even when I was a kid I played at being him. All the years I was a cop looking the other way from trouble I knew if I could just stay alive I would retire near here.

"I drove this truck from Chicago loaded with whatever would fit in – just like the days of the covered wagon – and with only the money from my first pension cheque in my pocket. I came up here to this place without knowing why, without thinking about it, before I even found a place to live. I slept out under the stars that night, right down there by those cottonwoods across the way from this car park.

And when I woke up the next morning I felt good – and *clean,* by damn – for the first time in years. I felt strong. I felt young. . ." His eyes started to get that mirror look.

"Shall I go in then?" I said. I didn't want him turning into Billy the Kid on me again before I'd even swallowed the first turn.

"Yes, go," he said. "Meet me down by the pond when you've had enough."

It didn't take me too long. I didn't like the feel of things in there, somehow. Soon I was walking along the banks of this kind of artificial slough, the kind they like to put in parks, wherever. Pond, they called it here. He was sitting at a park table, his back to me. He was making those motions that hand talkers use, the talkers who can't tell you anything without pointing fingers or rolling the air in front of them into balls or thumping their fists on tables and things like that.

At first I thought he was talking to somebody, somebody sitting in the shade of the big dark droopy cottonwood. And sure enough, as I came closer, I saw the figure of a boy, a teen-ager, I thought, or maybe a small man, almost hidden among the low-bent leaves of the cottonwood. He was wearing a hat – not a stetson, not a wide-brim, just a hat – like you see the guys wear on "Little House on the Prairies" and so on – and there seemed to be sparkly things here and there on it and on the rest of his clothes. I thought of rockers and their spiked hair or Elvis's nightclub jackets and kind of laughed to myself. If A.J. had a captive audience I just bet he was giving him particular what-for.

I got a little closer and there was nobody there.

"There you are," he said, "we've been waiting for you."

We sat in the sun under a sky so blue it hurt the eyes. I could not sit in the shade of that cottonwood. I tried, but it was like the cold storage at the Truck Stop, if you went in there without a sweater on even just long enough to pick up a can of lard for pie pastry you shivered big prickly shivers for quite a while when you came out.

A.J. was, well . . . *mellow.* We ate the last of the ham sandwiches I'd made from groceries I'd got after I'd ungrundged his fridge. Anything that was in there before I came could jolly well stay there and collect more green fuzz for all I cared – tomorrow I was up and gone. I'd brought tea in two thermoses. In one the tea was lukewarm, but what the heck, it was safe. We needed it all because this new, mellow Alphonse Joseph told me – told the ducks in the pond, really, or the reeds that grew green and tall along its banks – all the things he hadn't told me since I came.

I suppose my sister would call it typical dysfunctional family syndrome, or something like that: a father who skipped out early; a mother who worked too hard trying to keep body and soul together in the two of them; a marriage with a local girl who couldn't stand living with his mother – "a saint if ever there was one" – and who walked away taking their baby girl ; another marriage with a heart-o'-gold hooker (I kept wanting to say, "Aren't there any *bad* ones?" but thought better of it); she died the very next year.

When he got to the Filipino woman of the night before I oh-oh'ed to myself and dared to speculate whether he was carrying the little toy pistol and would show me again how "I should have shot her, right through her loud Woman's Lib mouth." They were "having it" – in the bathtub, of all places – he'd said, when she'd told him she was leaving. Maybe he figured it would be neater to kill her there; A.J. insisted often that he used to keep a very neat, clean house.

But he didn't do that, go off into a diatribe again. "I guess she had her reasons," he said now to the park's ducks. "She was only a kid, really. Nothing for her at home in that creepy place, people thicker than flies in the summertime there on those islands. I guess she saw him as a way out." He stopped talking.

Saw *him*? I said to myself. Saw *him*? Saw *who*?

"This man," he said, pointing to his own chest, "is the one I called here . . . " he motioned wide with one arm, "where I want to live. The essences are here, see? Not all the ones I knew then, but those who need to be here. Some call them ghosts; be that as it may, they know no better. There are many who come here to read those old words on old papers and they are caught by some faint remembrance. They do not know what it is, but they are stirred, somehow. They need to stay here but they do not know that and so they leave and squabble and make silly demands on the partner travelling in the Winnebago with them. The soul is trying to say: Stay here and correct some things of the past."

This could go on all night. How do I get out of this? Well, what the hell: "You're Billy the Kid. A.J.'s gone somewhere; *you're* Billy the Kid."

"Some call me that."

"What are you doing here?"

"I'm living. I am at peace."

"What's this thing with . . . this other guy?"

"A.J.? He is me in many ways even when he is awake and 'in charge'. In charge of nothing. He flails about. He hurts people, mostly himself."

"Why do you stay?"

"His vibrations are compatible to me. The most secure, precise match I've found. He loves me. He sees me in dreams and in the whiskey and in the heat of the sun. But I am almost always with him now."

I close my eyes now. I sit quietly. If I say nothing, it will all go away. *It is not really happening*. With luck I'll wake up and find I've never left North Battleford. Maybe it's

December still and there'll be snow to shovel. I'll shovel that snow as happy as a pig in you-know-what, just let me at it!

Behind the eyes I see somebody draw a pistol from under a grey cloak.

"We want something," he says. He is very deliberate.

I believe I am screaming, but I'm not sure. "Oh God, what? What do you want?" I open my eyes. He's still in the same position. There is no pistol, no cloak.

"*We want a son.*"

I swallow. Hard. Twice, at least, before I can get any words to come. "I wish you lots of luck," I say. For ten cents I would laugh.

"We want it from *you*," he says.

I may be laughing. I may be screaming. I may be crying. I may be as crazy as a loon. "I'm sixty years old!" I say.

"Miracles happen," he says. "Sleep with us tonight."

That's it. I've had it. "If you try anything funny tonight," I say, "I'll call a cop. A *real* one. Maybe even a doctor – and *he* can pay for it." I suddenly realize there's about as much chance of finding a cop or a doctor in happy little, green little, Truth or Consequences as there is of finding green grass under the oil pan of my old Toyota in December. "In fact," I say, "I'm not going one step further with him . . . with you . . . with you stupid jerks, so put that in your pipe and smoke it!"

There is silence. I stomp off. Then I stop. What the hell, it's all kind of pitiful. And I do have to get, somehow, to tomorrow's plane in Albuquerque. Then he is behind me, beside me. "It won't be necessary to do that," he says. "I would never hurt you; you're a *lady*. I would never let *him* hurt you, either. He will drive you back safely and he will apologize to you on the way home for his indelicate behaviour. He will be mostly me for the rest of the time you are here, in my New Mexico."

We stood silent in the hot sun. Then he stirred, took my arm, gently. I turned and looked him full in the face. "Are you all right, A.J.?" I said.

"Good as gold," he said. "Shall we go on home now and let those high fliers back in the coop for the night? It's getting on and there's a hawk lately taken to hanging around."

"Maybe you should be pitching the new eggs in the garbage," I said. "It's pretty loud advertising, having them grace your lawn. That hawk sees fried eggs in a pan and he comes looking for the meat that ought to go with them."

He laughed. "You see?" he said. "You should stay down here with me and boss me around. I'd like to be bossed by a little Canadian lady. I like 'em. I like Canadians."

On the plane going home I slept. I never thought I could ever do that, sleep on a plane. It's like if I go to sleep the pilot won't watch the road — you know what I mean? But this time I slept. And I had the clearest dream I 've ever had in my whole life.

My sister the school teacher was the stewardess. I had a window seat and I was watching the cloud-stuff below and thinking how much it all looked like a huge grain field in winter, with the snow rippled into furrows, sort of, covering the land and promising it good moisture to start the wheat in spring.

My sister the stewardess comes now and takes me by the hand. She leads me into the plane's cockpit. On the one side sits a little guy dressed in an Air Canada uniform but with a kind of flat old pioneer's hat on his head. He turns to me and grins. There is pain in it and I turn away. I do not want to look at him.

The pilot is a woman. She doesn't look at me. She keeps her eyes "on the road". She is about, oh, I'd say — it's hard to tell about these things, but something tells me I am supposed to know she is just about precisely thirty-three years old.

She is singing. There are no words, not even a tune you can remember and follow, but it is downright glorious.

"It's *you*, Rose," says my sister.

Who am I to doubt it? It's *my* dream, isn't it? And besides, she's wearing the long fleecy men's winter underwear I always wear (except in places like New goldarned hot old Mexico) when I go to bed.

PICTURES

As soon as she'd left Arthur Alfred, Emma got interested in sex. In the thirty-seven years she was married to him it was something done in the dark between hot sheets (or, in winter, between too often cold ones in the unheated bedroom of the A-frame farmhouse that hadn't seen even the insulation of a coat of paint since Arthur Alfred's father's time).

Arthur Alfred's "conjugular rights" were exercised rarely and, mercifully, quickly; they had become just another chore from the first time he availed himself of them three months after the wedding. Yet as soon as ever she left him, took the eight hundred dollars she had saved, mite by veriest mite, over twenty-seven years in a jam jar hidden in the pickle section of the cool cellar, and simply walked out to the grid and hitched a ride to Winnipeg with the Co-op fuel delivery truck, she got interested in sex.

She didn't even have the need to flip the switch in the mind that turns the words inside there off – turns *the* word off, might as well say. Turns the pictures inside there off too. She didn't have to do any of that because it all felt so good.

So all the way to Winnipeg she let the pictures roll about the Co-op fuel delivery man, whom she didn't know from Adam, who was at least twenty years younger and who spoke a lot about his wife and three kids and bet she had grandchildren to visit in Winnipeg, right? Well, he would just deliver their granny right to their very door and wouldn't they get a nice surprise? Somebody inside her then said: If you knew what I was seeing in my head right about now *you'd* be the one surprised! But she let him talk and she let the pictures roll and she smiled to herself about all the things the Co-op fuel man would never know.

She got him to let her off at Eaton's, the only place she really remembered. Once the truck door was slammed shut and she was standing on the sidewalk she didn't know what to do next so she found a telephone and looked up Doris's number and told her what she'd done.

Doris would have taken her in. "Sister or not," she'd said, as soon as the car door was closed with Emma in the passenger seat, "I kept out of it all these years. Though Mama must have turned over in her grave a hundred times the way that little pip-squeak made you work, milking cows by hand, if you please, and in this day and age."

"It's all right, Doris," Emma had said. "I like cows. I didn't mind." And then she closed her mind to Doris's talk, talk, talk and looked at the pictures. And an hour later Doris was still talking and there was a tea cup with tea in it in Emma's hand and she couldn't quite remember how it had got there. She drank a bit of it; it was still nice and hot. She placed the tea cup onto its saucer quietly. She had never liked noise of any kind. And Arthur, Arthur Alfred – he was named after two kings was Arthur Alfred and he often told you so – ever since his hearing wasn't what it used to be, Arthur did everything loudly.

He played the radio loudly to catch the morning news and weather; he ate his breakfast loudly; he grunted into his boots loudly; he gave her her orders for the day loudly; he banged the door the same way and started up the old truck with clatters and clangs and curses that penetrated the kitchen (quiet as soon as he'd left it) setting her teeth on edge, her heart a-flutter twenty times before he finally roared up the lane and was gone.

"I said you can come and live here," Doris was saying. "Can't you listen once? Fred won't mind; you know Fred!"

Emma knew Fred. Of course. Quiet, patient Fred. Who had milked cows for their father once. How quiet and peaceful it had been in the barn those times, just the two of them (and fifteen milk cows, of course!); she and Fred, one as tongue-tied as the other, so there was no chitter-chatter to invade the warm contented steaminess of quiet cows and clean straw and fresh new milk.

Until Doris would come barrelling in, yodelling as best she could like Wilf Carter at the top of her lungs, stealing Fred's cap to collect the eggs in, tying Emma's braids to the tail of the cow she was milking.

"Look, Freddie," she'd say, "Emma and old Jess are twins: you can't tell where one leaves off and the other begins."

"You shouldn't," Fred would say. But he would smile just a little, and Emma would feel awful, just awful. And he would get up off his milk stool and come over and undo the knot to free Emma's braids. And his hand would brush her hair sometimes, lightly.

And all too soon he and Doris were married and had moved into Winnipeg, all that way, and Papa bought them a little place.

"It was nice," she said now, placing a hand palm down over the tea cup to stop Doris from filling it again. "Your first little house. It was nice."

"Nice? It was a mousetrap. But I will say, Fred made good on the railway always, and as soon as ever I went to work at the hotel – not where I am now, I mean the old Fort Garry – well, it sure didn't take us long to pay Papa back and get something decent. I cleaned a lot of crappy toilets, let me tell you, to help do it. And Fred fixed and painted on the new place, and made his own lunches even going on the midnight if he had to and never once complained, you know Fred."

Emma knew Fred. And that's why she couldn't stay there. When Doris went gallivanting off to Bingo and she and Fred played cards or watched TV together it was all so quiet even if it was a shoot-'em-up they were watching and it was all so . . . well . . . *nice* that the pictures would start.

And the feelings. They might be playing cards and she'd be holding a nice hand, planning it out, when all at once the cards would just sort of flow one into the other and they would become a house right there in her hand. More like a cabana by the sea, maybe – whatever a cabana was. This one had a thatched roof and the rest of it was open to the sea and the sun and the salt breeze. And it had a hammock swaying gently from the beams. And she and Fred were in the hammock. Wearing not very much. Wearing, in fact, as she looked, nothing at all.

She hadn't seen Arthur Alfred in nothing at all in all the years they were together. Except in the bathtub when he yelled for her to come wash his back. And then he always had the washcloth spread out like a floating flower garden over his personals.

As if she would be so much as tempted to pluck his thorny rose!

But with Fred it was different, so she had to move out. Even though Doris said, "Don't. Where will you go? They won't even hire you to sew pockets in men's pants when you're just five years from the pension. Stay here, I tell you; if old A.A. comes looking, leave it to me to read him the riot act." Doris was good. The first thing she did when she came home off shift was to call "Emma!" and she never even stopped to take her coat off until she had tracked down where she was.

One of the good things about the city was a paper that came every single day. There were ads in it. Doris would read some of them out loud and laugh. "*Adventuresome male seeks like-minded*," she'd say. "I bet it's not the mind he's after!"

In Emma's mind danced pictures of a young couple, as sun-brown as in the TV ads with the colour turned up, dancing together on a golden beach, then sinking entwined – yes, the word had to be *entwined* – below white-capped waves, their bodies hot, hot despite the coolness of the water. She wasn't sure which of the bodies she was inside, but it didn't matter, she was there.

"A little adventure never hurt anybody," she said.

Doris rolled her eyes. "Listen to her," she said to Fred, "five years away from the pension and a regular innocent. In this day and age. Emma, it means he wants another *man*!"

The pictures on the TV screen inside Emma's head became a jigsaw puzzle and then made a new picture. The sun and the waves still felt good. "So?" she said. Doris did the eye roll again.

She read for a while silently, Doris did. Then she *tsked* her tongue loudly. "*You* better not read the want ads," she said, and put the paper aside. She hoisted her body out of the deep soft sofa and went to make tea. She brought it in on a wide tray along with real cream and with real sugar and with a high stack of raisin bread Emma had made that day, well-buttered and with sugar cinnamon sprinkled thickly over it.

In spite of herself Emma ate two slices. When the late news came on she sneaked the paper off with her to her room.

Every night Emma soaked in the deep tub in the white, white bathroom connected to her room. "It's yours, use it," Doris had said. "Soak the cow smell out of your pores – I know, I *know*, you *like* cows, you've said so a thousand times since you came."

And she'd rolled those famous eyes in the way that had always made their mother laugh and had driven the boys in the schoolyard to tease her so she would *tsk* her tongue, hands on hips, toss that head of gorgeous hair and give them the exasperated eye roll. "Go on, *fill* the tub," Doris had said, "enjoy it; baby yourself a little. Call me if you want your back scrubbed. Or Fred. He's good at it!"

The pictures, the feelings, the good smells of Fred doing that bothered her too much and she had to make her mind think of cows instead. It worked, until she felt again the firm-soft teats drawing the good warm white milk into the shining pail.

HOUSEKEEPER WANTED, FARM BACKGROUND PREFERRED. Emma knew she would phone the number in the morning as soon as ever Fred and Doris had gone to work. She saw the Wanter already: medium-tall, thickly muscled; clean-shaven, balding; neat as a pin; quiet-spoken. (In fact, Fred.)

Mr. Arnold was tall and skinny, actually, and he spoke loudly, with a lot of old country *eh wot? lass*'s and constant tinkering with his hearing aid. He had white bushy hair and white bushy eyebrows and a moustache that had once been a waxed military one, judging by the faded photos of him that hung everywhere on the walls of the sitting room. The moustache was now quite droopy and spilled over into Mr. Arnold's tea cup if he did not "exercise eternal vigilance over the demn thing!"

Mr. Arnold used a cane and was obviously relieved when Emma suggested she make the tea he offered. He went before her to the kitchen, whacking a swath through loose newspapers and empty grocery bags; in the kitchen he swung cupboard doors open with it, pointed out the "company tea things" with the tip of it, talking, talking, talking – *eh wot? lass* – the whole time. She thought he was kind of cute.

Emma would have liked a little hot buttered toast with the tea (she'd been too nervous to have anything that morning before she left), but she didn't want to be forward and suggest it. No milk, no sugar in the tea for Mr. Arnold, so she said she didn't take anything either.

Once back in the livingroom though, with its old-fashioned solid good wood and the deep plush large old sofas and chairs, every one antimacassered to the hilt,

Mr. Arnold smacked a round blue and silver tin box out from under a chair with the crook end of his cane. It said "Olde English Biscuits" on it and was, thankfully, half-full. Mr. Arnold, thankfully again, was quick to say, "Come, come, another one won't hurt you."

Mr. Arnold liked farm girls because he had worked on a farm when he came to this country and he had indeed married one of the farm daughters, bless her soul. He knew farm girls were clean and they were hard workers, *eh wot? lass.* Emma's mind didn't make a single picture of hammocks hanging from the roof beams of a cabana or of hot golden bodies entwined in the depths of cool-blue ocean waves, but she took the job anyway.

In fact, she stayed, then and there, and cleaned the bags and papers and old pizza cartons out of the kitchen in no time flat. He bungled about the kitchen the whole time whacking papers out of the way with his cane just as she bent to pick them up, bellowing, "Let me do that for you, *eh wot? lass*!" until she took the bull by the horns and said, "Now, Mr. Arnold, you're paying *me* to housekeep, remember? So how would it be if you sat right there in that nice Captain's chair and put your feet up and told me again what the sergeant-major said when they found out you were too young to be in the army, and when I'm done here we'll go for a walk together, what do you say?"

So they did that. They walked through a little park – Mr. Arnold was quite a walker; it was a good thing he was deaf and couldn't hear you puffing – and then they cut over to a little grocery store for "war supplies: against Hunger, the stalwart enemy". By then Emma was having a good time and the rest of the day flew by; she almost forgot to phone Fred and Doris; did, in fact, forget until Mr. Arnold offered her cab fare to go and get her things.

After she phoned they came so quick it was plain they hadn't even stopped for supper. "Well now, aren't you the cool one though?" Doris said when Emma answered the door. "Mama always said you were a deep one." But Doris didn't roll her eyes at Mr. Arnold or his gorgeous old house with the handsome shiny wood in it, she sat primly erect on a hard wooden chair, ankles crossed (to keep the skirt where it belonged, according to the rules laid down by Miss Caroline Warkentin in Grade Six in Clover Leaf School in northern Manitoba a good few years ago); she mouthed precisely the carefully chosen words she directed, well-modulated, Mr. Arnold's way so efficiently that he rarely had to twiddle with his hearing aid the entire evening.

Fred sat quietly, of course. And smiled and winked at Emma (she had hammock pictures the minute he did that) and hooked a thumb in sly look-at-*them*-will-you? style in the direction of Doris and Mr. Arnold now loudly enjoying the old military photographs on the wall, each one-time buddy reminisced about being smacked soundly on the head by Mr. Arnold's cane. He ignored Fred and Emma completely, except to whack the biscuit tin into view from beneath a chair and suggest Emma make tea.

So she forefingered Fred into the kitchen with her and made ham sandwiches to go with the cookies, starting Fred off with a big thick one, light on the mustard, before she even plugged in the kettle for tea.

By the time Mr. Arnold was booming, "Come again! Come again!" all the while hanging on to Doris's hand so tight she almost never got to go, let alone come again, it was late news time *eh wot? lass*, but all Emma wanted was to close the door on herself in the cozy big room on the third floor that had once belonged to Mr. Arnold's studious third daughter. Who was also good and practical, for she had had the huge hall-closet-that-once-was made into a young lady's modern-day bathroom with her first salary cheque from the library. Because she said she was going to live with her parents forever.

"Never so much as took a bath in the bathtub," Mr. Arnold said. "Maybe never so much as looked at her pretty self in the fancy mirror." She had been struck down by a speeding motorist running a yellow light – "They all drive here like Parisians, demn them all," Mr. Arnold said – and she never opened her eyes again though Mr. and Mrs. Arnold took turns and stayed with her every minute of the twenty-seven days it took her to die.

"*She* never called it *dying*," Mr. Arnold said. "The missus never called it *dying*, she said you *translated* to other worlds, but then, she was one of them Spiritualists, bless her, they're rife as weeds in a flax field in this town. I myself could never understand them. But once our baby was gone her mum simply decided she wasn't staying behind and so she up and off too, just like that, not even a headache when she went to bed. She just said, 'I'm going off to Melba tonight, William, forgive me.' And she slipped away like smoke in the wind and with a smile on her face."

The droopy moustache had drooped even more limply as Mr. Arnold told that story while they waited for the kettle to boil once they'd got home from their afternoon walk with the war supplies. There was so much of everything – pictures, sounds, smells, feeling – spinning through Emma that whole first day that now, with Doris and Fred safely gone, all she wanted, and what she very much needed, was to slip out of her clothes and at once into the cool-blue waves of the blue cotton bed-ocean and let it all roll her into a sleep that would have no room for cows or the farm life she had left behind.

Or for Arthur Alfred, whose loudness was of a different order from Mr. Arnold's. Mr. Arnold's did not set the teeth on edge. At least not yet. Six months later she had heard the same war stories so many times she could put herself on automatic, like the fancy oven Doris had taught her to use, and cook supper to the tune of Mr. Arnold's loud voice and be ready to set it on the table with his last *but we showed the blighters, eh wot? lass*. By now, too, she knew every nook and cranny of at least a good quarter-section of Winnipeg around Mr. Arnold's place because they walked a good part of it every day, his cane whacking stray Colonel Sanders' boxes and sections of discarded newspapers and even unwary cats and dogs out of the way. Once he let fly at a child's abandoned go-cart and she had visions immediately of a child having been in it, but of course that wasn't so.

Then she began wondering what Mr. Arnold had looked like, felt like, in his hammock days. She began looking at the ads again, but she didn't really want to leave Mr. Arnold's handsome old house with the third-storey room full of studious books. Not that Emma read any of them, but she liked the feel they gave the room, as if they were pleasant and kindly people waiting for the translated daughter to visit with them again.

Sometimes, if Mr. Arnold's cronies had been there all evening playing poker and smoking up a storm, Emma's head felt as though it at least wanted to "translate" somewhere else, it didn't care where, as long as it was away from tobacco smoke. At first she'd been pleased to be asked to play, to be coached from all sides of the table and allowed to get away with murder as far as the rules were concerned. It was even kind of exciting to have all these old men telling you how quickly you caught on and offering to put up the nickels for you.

Eventually though, the smoke got to her, and lately, back in the safe upper storey, the door closed tightly, the window open to spring and to its apple blossoms, there were . . . well . . . *visitors* who came wafting in with the fragrances of the night and they became so real somehow that their voices began to ring in her head.

First they were simply the replayed voices of the card players saying over and over again: *Don't go yet, Emma, it's early!* But as she sat silently there came into her the voices of others – maybe even of Mr. Arnold's good daughter – saying: *Leave here! Go, go, go, go, go!*

She didn't really want to, but she started reading the newspaper ads again. There was no feeling of any kind, only a dullness of the heart, when she was reading the Help Wanted kind, but one night, her head filled with poker smoke, her eyes happened to fall on COMPANIONS WANTED and in less than a snap of the fingers her heart welled wide in her chest almost to bursting. For she could hear, could see him, a man of medium height, with greying hair, lots of it; dressed in a blue-grey suit, a three-piecer; saying in quiet, kindly tones: *Are you a mature lady who puts friendship at the head of the list but isn't afraid of a little adventure? Let's make a new life together; age, colour, and status no problem; I'm an Equal Opportunity Friend! Phone number, please.*

Then and there she sat down at Mr. Arnold's daughter's beautiful pale oak desk and wrote to the man. She never for one minute thought he might not answer.

For three weeks the time flew again and she even began listening once more to Mr. Arnold's war stories, saying, "Well, you don't say!" or "Who would have thought it?" in all the right places. Then one morning very early, Mr. Arnold's daughter's phone rang, the phone Mr. Arnold now called Emma's phone.

But it was Doris. "Arthur Alfred is after you," she said. "Finally, after all this time, he phones. I bet he has another woman on the hook because he's threatening divorce unless you come back; he's just looking for a way around things –

nowadays they have to give you half. Get yourself a lawyer and don't let him wiggle out."

It seemed as though all that belonged to somebody else. "Does he know where I am?" Emma said. It somehow seemed she ought to say *something*.

"Are you crazy? What do you take me for? I said we hadn't seen you; I said he'd better try his girls."

Emma's heart turned over. Topsy-turvy completely. She even saw it, a valentine heart, flopping itself end to end so that its rounded shoulders were bottom and its sharp bottom point was now the top and sticking like a knife-point into her breastbone. She hadn't thought of Arthur Alfred's daughters in a long, long time.

"He said he *wrote* them long ago," Doris said. "Leave it to good old A.A.; he wouldn't get loosened up enough to phone long distance unless there was money waiting at the other end guaranteed to pour gold out at his end. He was in Winnipeg, he said, to pick up a new Honey Wagon; maybe he hopes you'll hear the good news and be impressed. If you go back to that miserable excuse for a louse, Emma, I swear to God I'll never forgive you!"

"It's all right," Emma said. "Mr. Arnold has been asking when you're coming to see him."

"For God's sake, Emma, this is *important*! What are you gonna *do*? What are *we* gonna do?"

"Now Doris, listen; give me an answer; I promised Mr. Arnold I'd ask the next time you called." Emma saw pictures of Doris's mind. It was scattered lightning. Red. No, maybe the colour was more like scarlet.

Then the lightning turned blue and Doris said, "Oh, I don't know . . . I get so bored with the poor old fart, make me some excuse, eh? I don't want to hurt his feelings . . . I mean . . . oh for God's sake, why are we talking about Mr. Arnold? Are *you* OK?"

"Yes," said Emma. She looked around the large bright room. The window curtains were a pale gold in the early morning sun; the books on the many shelves wished her kind words; outside, reaching towards her window, new apples were forming on sound limbs.

Mr. Arnold's daughter's room was becoming hers and she did not want to leave it, even to go below and cook Mr. Arnold's old-fashioned oatmeal breakfast, or even to walk alone in the large greening garden in the early morning sun.

But she did those things anyway. She put Arthur Alfred out of her mind.

And that night the man phoned. She almost didn't answer. She thought at first that maybe Arthur had tracked her down, but how could he have, the phone wasn't listed in her name. But maybe Doris gave in? Or Fred? The thoughts scatter about your head so, like lightning dancing on a white wire fence in a late summer storm while the phone rings once . . . twice . . . three times.

You reach over as in a dream, as if it is another *you* doing it, ready to say to Arthur . . . well, you don't know what . . . and he says (his voice is like a movie star's or a TV preacher's), "Emma? I'm so looking forward to meeting you."

They met at McDonald's. He was so good-looking, so neat and clean and so smiling. And so quiet. So Emma knew at once he was the Companion she had wanted all her life. The hammock pictures did not even put themselves to the trouble.

He asked if they could go to her place so they could talk better. Emma said, well, she kept house for an older man, but the kitchen there was very nice, how about that? And he said, No, no, no, that really wouldn't do, they might be interrupted.

That made sense. Emma said, "Well yes, it's true Mr. Arnold is quite a talker and if he comes in and gets started on the last three wars that's the end of an evening right there. So how about where you live?"

And the man said, well, he had this teen-age son and no telling when he might walk in the door.

And Emma said, "I'm looking forward to meeting him."

And the man said, well, the kid was still all upset about the divorce and it could be quite a disturbance, right?

And Emma said, "Well, let's walk in the park then and talk, shall we?"

And the man said there were often bad people in parks – drunks and pushers, the world was going to the dogs for sure. "But look," he said, "I really, really am drawn to you, don't you know some place we can go?"

She took him to Doris and Fred's. It was a week both worked days. And the man got very fond and for a while it felt very hammocky and everything, although there weren't any pictures. But all at once Emma didn't feel good about it and she said, "It's too early, it's too quick; I wanted a friend first."

But it happened anyway. And it was really no different than with Arthur. And Emma offered to make tea so they could really talk and get to know each other, but the man had an appointment and had to go.

"Maybe we can talk on the phone sometime then?" Emma said. "I have lots of time at night."

"Sure," the man said. "I'll give you a call."

"Or you could leave me *your* number," Emma said.

"That doesn't seem to work," said the man. "I live with these teen-agers, and you know how these kids are, always hanging on the phone; I wouldn't put you to the trouble."

"It's no trouble at all," Emma said.

"No, no, no," the man said, "it's best if I do the calling."

And he was gone.

She knew his first name. That was all. Well, and his face. And how he fit in a hammock, you might say. The words about that surprised Emma so, she had to smile in spite of herself.

She had a shower. Scoured herself with lots of lather. She washed the bedsheets and re-made the bed. Somehow she still smelled the good clean man smell of him. She locked the house behind her carefully, stowed the key carefully in a zippered side pocket of her purse – she'd promised Doris to take good care of it always – and found a bus to take her back to Mr. Arnold's place.

Three weeks later the man still hadn't called. The only pictures she was having lately were of gardens, green and diamond-sparkled with dew, and with flowers she didn't know splashed gold and crimson and purple slap-dash throughout the greenness.

Then, at breakfast, she was surprised to hear herself asking Mr. Arnold if she could have two weeks off for a holiday. "Not that living here isn't a holiday!" she added, surprising herself again.

She had found once more the paper Doris had given her with the lawyer's name on it. Her bank book she left behind and anything new she had bought since she'd come to Winnipeg. She took a cab to the bus depot and gave the driver two dollars for himself too.

She didn't phone Doris. She would do that, long distance, from the farm.

As she got on the bus she bet herself ten dollars there was an electric milking machine now in the barn.

RUNNING HOT AND COLD

I am 57 years old today, and, for the first time in my life, on the threshold of passion. I have "found my man", and the Country songs are dead right "on" about the feeling.

I am 57 years old today. And 5+7=12. And 1+2=3. And 3= the holy trinity: the Father, Son, and Holy Ghost. (All right, all right: the Mother, Child, and Holy Spirit.)

But wait a minute, even that one isn't right; doesn't go far enough. The 3 *really* = The Mind-of-all-*things*; the little lowly childish individual mind; and the Holy Ghost of All-Mind (better called spirit): there you are, chapter and verse for today. I haven't lived 57 years in a vacuum, though there have been some to say I have lived them with my head in the clouds. That was my mother. She said I was too much like my father. So I have lived the outer life carefully, trying to be as little as possible like my mother. Which helped her to reiterate every time she saw me: You are too much like your father, do you know that?

Not that it matters. I am 57 years old today and on the threshold of passion: the overpowering demands of the flesh. So I have no business today to be thinking about the old ones who live across the alley from me. Not a stone's throw away. I could almost spit onto the Golden Sunset's impeccable green lawns, its small round garden (the holy circle of ever-on-going life, ha!) where its old ones are encouraged to plant four hills of potatoes in spring, or six pea seeds, or six marigolds, in the radius rows assigned to them.

I am 57 years old today and have no business to be thinking about the old ones who totter in baggy beige trousers, on worn earth-coloured carpet slippers, about the perambulating rough cement paths of the Golden Sunset's personal private park, wearing their soles more ragged still. I have no business to watch them.

To watch them being walked too fast, too fast, by those who are too young and therefore should not be in charge of those who are too old to walk alone.

Too fast, too fast. Haven't I been watching one too long now, disciplining one draggy foot after the other up the rough cement incline to the back door? It took him twelve minutes by the clock to do so.

They would not let him in. He was waved away by a large young one who knows how to use sign language, body language, no-nonsense body language very well. He was waved away because another younger one was already tracking him, having whipped his baggy beige sweater about her white uniformed shoulders, for it is raw out this too early fall morning, though two days ago we sweltered under a blistering sun.

Here she is now. The beige-sweatered one. She zips the sweater from her own shoulders, slings it about his, adjusts it to fit partly over her own, and then takes his elbow to steer him back down the rough cement incline, away from the glass door he has no business to be tapping against. He resists. Tugs at the sweater. She insists. Snugs it about them again. He slips, nearly falls into the meagre spirea guarding the back door. He seems to be saying something. I hope it is, "I want to *wear* the damn thing, Stupid!"

In any case, she whips it from his shoulders and whips it again – this time like a sail behind the two of them – then whips it up his arms, extended in anticipation now behind him like the wings of a wild goose about to take off in fall for Florida, or wherever it is Saskatchewan wild geese take off to.

They have obviously been through this sweater routine before, these two non-fliers, for each knows what to do.

But now she is cold, naturally (for isn't *he* now wearing the sweater?), and so she hustles him slipslopslipslopslipslop too fast for worn carpet slippers over the meandering rough walks, past the various Pioneers, Oh Pioneers! miniatures – buckboards and covered wagons and what-have-you's – that decorate the green-green unblemished lawn.

"Do they draw them at sundown into a circle against marauders?" Paul asked. Someone from the Golden Sunset had hitched his little green garden tractor to one of the covered wagons and was getting into loud gear to haul it somewhere. Paul's woman had just left him. He was here with me, I knew, because his psyche had needed to remember the one who had once told him he had the secret smile of a sexy Trappist monk.

We were on the balcony overlooking the "park" the old folks' home brochures promise prospective "family members". I have seen the brochures; they address them-selves entirely to the ones who will commit somebody to "a golden sunset at Golden Sunset", and really, what's so wrong about that?

Anyway, I've no business with that. Paul and I were on the balcony. We were eating cherries. Or I was. He was eating and drinking nothing. He was not even breathing anymore. Or so it seemed to me, wanting him, and watching him watch the horizon, or nothing, maybe, over the grey rooftops of the low-slung Golden Sunset Home with the rather startling huge and scarlet G S H spelled out on top of it in roofing tiles.

I'd just told him to buck up and force himself to go on living or else totter across to the Golden Sunset and make his application. "Here," I said, offering him a denuded cherry pit, "toss it across and claim your place on the church pew park bench. Then go sit on it and hope it will act like a thumbtack where it will do the most good. Because a man who feels obliged to mourn for a woman dumb enough to give up a sexy Trappist needs more than a kick in the slats. He needs a reminder he's only mortal, after all."

"All too," he finally said.

"And for not nearly long enough," I said. I was still holding the cherry pit.

He turned to me; I waggled the cherry pit at him; he took it and hefted it towards the Golden Sunset park bench. It missed.

He stood for a long time looking off into space in the general direction of the toss. Then the fingers of one hand began tapping a light tattoo on the balcony railing. "I guess maybe I could handle that beer now," he said.

I brought him tea, strong, and cheese and toast instead. Sugar in the tea. Lots of it. And more black cherries still wearing a flash of red. After he had the cheese and toast safely inside him I poured brandy into more hot tea and scolded him to drink it as hot as he could stand it.

Then he talked. And talked and talked and talked. The sun set and the stars came out and poured sweet sure energy on us where the man I had loved for twenty years sat talking, talking about the only woman he had ever loved – on my balcony with the secure wrought-iron railing and overlooking the place where old ones lie, nights, remembering, perhaps, the murmur of voices behind secure bedroom doors, going on and on far into the comforting night.

Before the sun came up he asked to go to bed with me. Instead, I put him to rest with more hot brandy in the big double bed where I never sleep myself, and huddled alone under cold polyester sheets on the cot I sleep on beside my desk in the workroom because a narrow bed does not remind you as often that you are sleeping alone.

I don't know what makes for such perversity in a woman who has lived alone for far too many years. What would it have hurt me to have given him the comfort of another body in that bed?

I don't know why I do the things I do. There was a young woman who came to see me once because she had heard I was a witch. I felt a sure charge of fear dead to the heart when she told me that. I could see myself, then and there, being burned at the stake like Joan of Arc; see myself/feel myself being flailed along with the Salem women. But I laughed heartily and said, "What a peculiar notion!" to the woman who had come calling. And before she left she read tea leaves for me and said they told me to stop being everybody's Earth Mother; to opt, instead, for passion. And I laughed again because the man I had loved for nearly twenty years was living secure with a woman who was witch and mother-goddess and mistress-bitch – and what Trappist in his secret heart of hearts could want any more than that? And so, so much for the tea leaves' passion.

Besides, what is this *passion*? A tarot card reader had promised it to me years and years ago, before I believed in myself, let alone such things as tarot card readers or other assorted gypsy types. Then I met a hermit who lived alone by a lonely lake where the free energy was so concentrated you could hear it sing when you walked into the bush with him to cut wood. You could hear it whistle. You could, in fact, feel it zip-tingle the ears.

The hermit was a self-confessed astrologer. I could have given myself to him in passion. With passion. Because of passion. I was ready to, and I wanted to. He laid out my life for me on paper one night, sitting late beside the small tin heater devouring the wood we had that day cut. His paper said a soul mate would in this life be denied me. Unfortunately, he believed in his own divinings. Perhaps more unfortunate, he had decided, somewhere within himself, that passion was the sole prerogative of soul mates, and so he offered me that night his mind instead.

I met him again, years later. He had been cutting wood so long by then, the semen seed had left the sacred sac in him one winter morning early, he told me; it had travelled up the spine to his head, transmuting itself on the journey into pure blue energy which seared through his cranium in two places – right brain, left brain – and fused then into a blue-silver arc (neighbours who came calling had seen it and reported it to him) above his head.

There is no future in longing after the flesh of an astrologer who has a passion for blue-silver energy, I told myself then, and disciplined myself to learn to love myself earnestly within the confines of my own single bed.

Not too long after that I sold my house. It had far too many rooms. I was 55 years old. 5+5=10; 1+0=1; 1= the perfect, unified whole. (Astrologers, it seems, are of some use, after all.)

My perfect, unified whole had suddenly felt too old to scrape paint, to kill dandelions, to barter with pot-bellied "handymen" (ALL WERK GARNATEED) for the replacement of basement windows knocked in, each time I had to be away on the road, by ten-year-old kids looking for loose change for the arcade machines two blocks from my "private property" home.

My mind had said to me one morning back then – said it very clearly, said it *too* clearly for one who is afraid of being burned some day at the stake: *Look up; look down; live high and green and joyously free!* And when I found this apartment high on a hill near the river and overlooking a small cool-green park with wandering paths and an assortment of little covered wagons promising, in a way, a trek into new bold territory, I never stopped to ask who all that clipped and combed greenery belonged to, but paid quickly a year's rent so that, from my balcony window, it could – undandelioned and green and fruitful – belong exclusively to me.

Of course, the day I'd come looking, they'd kept all the beige old ones inside; not a one of them slip-slopped, shoulders hunched and chin hunched to watch for gravel stones on the hard cement walk, to warn me of what I would soon become, having known no passion save the passion of the mind.

How many times have I loved that pure-energied hermit on the woven raw-wool rug beside his hot hungry tin heater? Inside the mind. How many times have I indulged the over-hot heart, the over-heated vessel, with the man I have loved for twenty years, in an unmosquitoed green bower in the garden of his woman, in fact, almost under her very nose?

When the passions-of-night were done, those times, I was never required to speak on the subject of "How was it, sweetheart?" or "Be honest, was it good for you too?" I never had to fetch cold orange juice or hot brandy to revive one, passion-spent, who allowed as how it was just too hot to keep his arm around me any longer, or even his hand in mine.

I did not have to say, "Just a little more, please, please," to one whose semen seed was considering transmuting itself to blue-silver energy rather than be called upon once more in this demanding life of the flesh.

Women who have lived alone too long are just too perverse for words.

What memories do those beige ones across the alley have in their narrow beds at night? Were they fetchers of brandy and orange juice, or were they the consumers, the ones who have been fetched to all of their passionate lives?

Evolution, I am told, is a sure and a careful thing. Before the perfect, unified, single whole there must first arise the perfect, unified, *partnered* whole. For long enough to set the pattern. For long enough to learn about perfect passion from it: no fetchers and carriers, only an ever-onflowing give-give-give.

The last three nights Paul has phoned me. I have known for a long time that the name *Paul* means *little*: when it is your job to inspire aspiring ones to know the reason for every syllable they place in a poem, you soon teach yourself to believe in the meanings of words.

Little.

Passion.

Little passion.

The last three days I have spent the hours listening to the little passions of the perambulating old ones, watching – vulnerable, behind the wrought-iron rail of a third-floor balcony – *un*passioned gaze fixed steadfastly on the next tottery step on a rough cement walk.

Each time Paul has phoned I have told him I have students coming and that we shall be working late.

If he phones again tonight perhaps I shall tell him to fetch along a bottle of brandy and come.

THE NEW WORLD'S HOME

I can tell you one thing: they weren't all of them the Pioneers! Oh Pioneers! types, and that's God's truth on it.

Some were shiftless; some were witless; some were plain useless and stupid. And some were ordinary men with their fair share of brain and muscle, but luck stood against them: hail clobbered the wheat or the sun burned it blacker than Toby's arse after it had headed out and grown plump and good; there was no money left after you'd paid four hundred dollars apiece for foundered horses, and there was no way to make any more cash, either; there were too many kids and a wife so homesick she could hardly see straight half the time.

Oh I tell you, there were lots didn't make it on the bold bad prairie – well ya, in the bush country too; of course, in the bush country, I've got a story about that too – and I had a great-granddad was one of them that didn't make it.

He was a Jew, so they say; that was the first of it. Brainy. You know how that would go over in the old days – I don't mean the old days here, I mean the old days back in Europe, Germany, where he came from – if you lived amongst nothing but peasants who knew you couldn't eat books and the best thing you could give anybody was a strong back and willing hands.

Anyway, the old story in our family is that he was a Jew – and maybe my mother made it up, I don't know, because the first time that ever I heard it was when I was giving a buddy of mine the gears because he had to go to Hebrew school on a Saturday and my mother said it was only by the grace of God I got to go to the garbage dump the same day with my dad and bring home old junk to clutter the yard, because I had some Hebrew in me too, so just watch it, Mister!

That's the way she was, my mother.

But anyway, this old guy, this old great-granddad, back there in Germany, he married the handsome youngest daughter of a poor farmer from what they called the Pfalz. Woodland and hills and what not. Like the Black Forest, everybody knows the Black Forest; well, the same thing was the Pfalz. Nice. I never been there but I've heard it's really nice.

This was in the 1800's somewhere, and she was nearly twenty years younger and too handsome by far, so the story goes. Well, I suppose, handsome for the times, know what I mean? Because there were pictures of her in an old shoe box – old stuff my dad kept and never looked at – and we kids used to giggle ourselves silly, rainy Saturdays, at the goofy ancestors. If you wanted to get my sister Irma all fired up, you just told her she was a dead ringer for *Grossmutter* Hedwig and you sure had a fight on your hands.

So anyway, this great-grampa on my dad's side, his name was Ludwig; Ludwig Wilhelm Reinoldo Wuchert. And he married Hedwig Ludwig; funny, eh? And the trouble started right then and there. Because he'd promised her old man they would farm, see? Not that the old man had land to give them, because he didn't, they had only these little plots and always too many kids and *et cetera*; you know how it goes.

So there was this king. Sort of a king. Maybe the son of the ruling empress or something. And this, where this ruler is ruling, is in a part of the old country – Europe, I mean – that's Poland now, but used to change hands oftener than laundered money on its way to a Swiss bank.

There wasn't much to being a king back then in some of those places, you know. You had maybe half a section of land – lots of times less; I mean, how much was there to start with? (Just go look at a map and compare it to Saskatchewan.) So you had a little chunk of land and a big stone house on it, likely high on a hill by a river. So you were safe there and could keep your sheep – and, I suppose, your daughters – safe behind stone walls or a moat or whatever. And so you prospered. And so after a while people started calling you a king or a baron or so on and said that you lived in a castle. I got me some pictures of some of those castles when I was in the War. They were some disappointment, I can tell you.

Anyway, this olden times king, the one from Poland or whatever, he heard about these hardworking Germans back there in the *Pfalzer Wald* boondocks and how they could make wheat and barley grow practically out of sand, and he sent word for as many as wanted to come on out to his place, to do just that. He'd have land for them, and houses too. (I wouldn't be surprised his fingernails were scraping the bottom of the treasury box and so it was a prime idea, if you owned a country's worth of land, to bring in a few more peasants to pay rent and taxes.)

So OK, they went. They went from their little hard-pressed plots there in the Pfalz by foot and cart and wagon, as far as the Danube; then it was by boat to Vienna, and then by foot again, two hundred miles to this Promised Land. Twelve thousand families. Not twelve thousand people, twelve thousand families. And when they got there there were fifty-eight houses for the lot of them!

So I guess Ludwig Wilhelm Reinoldo could be mighty glad he'd refused to load up and go with Hedwig's papa. He went to Canada instead. Oh yes, Hedwig went to work – this was while they were still there in the Pfalz – taking in washing, or something (when nobody knows what somebody did for a living they always say they took in washing, have you ever noticed that?) and Ludwig himself, he kept on being some kind of low-order clerk of the court. Anyway, they laid by some cash, just enough to get here, and then they took a ship to Canada. In my dad's old shoe box was a folded-up piece from a German newspaper of the day promising those gullible peasants they would be eating peaches off their own trees out of their own orchards three years after they planted them. Peach trees! In *Saskatchewan*!

I didn't believe the story myself until I retired and then I kept getting curiouser and curiouser about this family stuff and so I had the German stuff in my dad's box all translated.

Well, what I started to say, about these old pioneers, it wasn't just the Germans got dinged by the real estate and the travel people. The Poles and Russians and Ukrainians (they used to lump them all together and call them Galicians, the early Anglos here did) they got soaked in too, of course. But the thing of it is, the British did too! Sure they did. And this was their own country back then. In a manner of speaking.

There was more green English bachelors than anything else in this neck of the woods for quite a good few years, my dad used to say. More than there was buffalo, that's for sure, they were long gone by then. Only their bones left. An old picture of my granddad – not my dad's dad, my mother's – there he is standing with a goldarn hunting rifle beside a stupid great pile of white buffalo bones, his foot up and resting on a big skull! That was when he made a trip out to the prairies from Jolly Old to "look the place over". There he is with one foot up on a buffalo skull.

Like the Great White Hunter. Africa. The Veldt. All that stuff. What else could you expect? He was one of them. One of them who came out to the Colonies for a bit of adventure and to make a fortune and to prove to the folks at home that he did have it all aced after all.

He never made it, either. He took homestead in solid bush. The green woods of home, and all that. Found some of his stuff in my dad's shoe box too; my mother didn't keep such things, she said she had enough pictures in her head about the old days – all of them bad – to last her a lifetime.

Can you imagine cutting your ten acres per year out of solid bush? And with a hand axe! You had to clear ten acres a year, see? To get the land. The land wasn't *free*, my god. True, you paid only ten bucks up front, but that was a filing fee, and what you paid after that was whatever it took to clear ten acres a year for three years. And live there for six long months of each year.

Some lottery, eh? My mother's dad, he didn't make it. He tried. Left his family there one winter and walked to town to get work. Drayman. He was good with horses. Walked back to the homestead with grub, basics, once a month. The cow died. One of the kids too. My mother said once he felt worse about the cow – it didn't cost fifty dollars to get another kid.

Anyway, he didn't make his three years, his commitment. He gave it up – the land, the dream, the plans to be king of all he surveyed (well, what you could survey from the back-door of a tarpaper shack in that bush country wasn't one whole hell of a lot, admit it) – gave it all up and moved the family to town. And my grandma, a plucky big woman from Leeds, used to work in the factories when she was only a bit of a girl – she made hats for the local women. Milliner, they called it. And he, Granddad, he kept an eye on the cookie jar, you might say, where she put the bits and pieces of change left over from the house expenses. And that's what set them up in the livery business.

Oh yes, the livery business. That seemed to run through both sides of the family, for some reason. On my dad's side there was that old German Ludwig (well naturally, he wasn't old when they came here, it's just a way of saying things), he was so green ignorant, being so bookish and dreamy, he couldn't even harness a horse himself, he had to get her – Hedwig, the wife – to do it.

They'd managed to buy a buggy – no, no, now, I'm wrong: it was a two-seater, a democrat; they called the two-seaters a democrat, at least where *we* lived. And he drove around to the different places, the farms and villages, with things the people might need: needles, thread, knives, salve (salve for people, salve for horses), things like that.

And he did OK on that, from the sound of things, but he never learned how to harness a horse, I guess he didn't have room in his head for it. And his team wore their collars – I mean their whole rig and regalia, of course – sometimes for a week, so the story goes. You know these old stories: one part truth and the rest whatever will make them perk up their ears at night in the bunkhouse.

That's what they said, anyhow. That his horses sometimes carried their harness for a week until he got home and got Hedwig to do it . . . Later the boys; they had seven of them altogether; six girls too, so there was something new the old fellow didn't mind learning, eh? When they got back to the home stall was when those poor old nags got combed and curried and had their shoulder sores salved up (with hog's lard and sulphur, not the tinned salve that got sold on the road, that cost money). Ya, so it goes, so it goes.

So like I said, they never made it on the farm. They *lived* on the farm, mind you. Not the homestead. They lost the homestead. But you could buy land, sometimes the best land in the district, cheap. Lots of ways. And if you owned your land you didn't have to clear even an acre in all the time you owned it, if you didn't want to; it was yours and you could do with it what you wanted – or at least what you could. And even an acre of turnips and potatoes and beets and onions can get a big family through the winter.

Winter wood was the thing. But the neighbors took pity, I guess, when they'd see Hedi, swelling again with a new one under the apron and out sawing wood with the short bucksaw her papa had made in earlier times in the old country; I've got it to this day. Or *had* it, I should say, till I broke this hip and had to give up the farm and move into this place. Nice enough place, but not for me, I'd rather be bucking my own wood yet for morning exercise with Gramma Hedi's queer little old saw. Ya, man, Gramma Hedwig's little old saw with the hooked nail where a good bolt is supposed to be. I never put a bolt back in. I don't know, but to see the nail she'd put in in a pinch, always . . . well, it made me feel for her every time. And maybe that's not a bad thing, to feel for the ones who are of the blood that made you.

She was a great old girl. Bit by bit she and the kids made a farm. Market garden, we say today. Ludwig sold the stuff off the democrat. Then from a wagon, later. One of the boys along to harness and drive the horses and to lift things, the old guy in a tie and bowler hat and white collar. So help me! Later they had a store in town. Or he did.

Hedwig never left the farm. A couple of the boys were a good help, and there wasn't a lot phased any of her girls, I can tell you. And there was a hired man for over thirty years. He died then, still on the farm. Still in service, you might say.

She was a sturdy one, that Hedwig. Nearly twenty years younger than the old storekeeper, did I mention that? You know what *that* means.

Aw, come on! See this picture? The whole fam damily there. *Except* Papa Ludwig. And *in*cluding the hired man. You get me now all right, eh?

And there, that's Hedi's youngest, my own grampa, handsome as they come, riding the hired man's shoulders.

Yes, she did all right on that farm, did Hedwig, and Ludwig did just fine in the selling business, but he sure as all hell was no pioneer like they like to tell about in the movies or in the local history books where everybody seemed to spend every day of their lives fighting the land and the grasshoppers and the weather and the coyotes. Some just figured out what was needed by those who were doing all those other things and supplied it and so they hung in there and made it through; the others just figured out the whole kit and kaboodle wasn't worth a tinker's dam and they gave up and high-tailed it somewhere else: B.C., the States, back to the old country or back to old Ontario.

And there were a lot more than you'd ever suppose, just like that. The ones who didn't hang in. We just don't seem to want to tell those stories, or even to remember them. I guess it spoils the idea we've got about ourselves as the sprigs of some romantic pioneering bush. If the bush didn't take root we don't want to know it; or, if we know it, we don't want to tell it. And that's a fact.

AND SO IT GOES

Here it was: Deutschland. Not *über alles*, not a rushed flowering of some latent genetic feeling for an ancestral nation, just green wooded hills and ancient castles along the rivers, and flowers, dear heaven, *Blumen*, *Blumen*, everywhere – in the parks, in the fields, along the railway tracks, in people's gardens. And in the window boxes – homes, businesses, government offices, schools: their sound wooden window boxes held geraniums, pinks, whatevers!

If you are by nature, speculated Ulla, as unadventurous as a woods violet, you are content where you are – where you were born, and where your good-enough-for-me mind-set has kept you. And so you get to be sixty years old before you know where you really belong.

There had been other places she had been to. Dragged to. Pushed into. By friends; by temporary lovers, sometimes; by a practical, practiced hassler who seemed to live in the left-hand side of the head – just behind the left eye, in fact – who kept saying: *You'll soon be old, and where will you have been? Saskatchewan, that's where! A few miles this way, a few miles that way; so get up off your self-satisfied sitter and go someplace!*

There'd been Mexico. Mexico had been with an old boyfriend – or somebody who would have been a boyfriend if she had let him kiss her at that weiner roast at Blueberry Pines when they were in Grade Eight. They'd come across each other again when he'd been twice married and twice divorced (well, *nearly* so, the second time). In Mexico she had discovered Quetzalcoatl interested her more than a man with artificial teeth who refused to wear a sheath during crucial encounters because he said it was like washing your feet with your socks on.

The night they'd got back to Saskatchewan he had stayed long enough to shake his finger gently at her over all the little things he disapproved of in her personality and in her behaviour. When the door closed behind him she was shut of him. She sent back his ring by registered mail, let the phone ring itself off the wall for three solid weeks, zipped any letters from him into the junk mail box for delivery to the paper recycling bin in the city, one of which she got back with a nice note from a sentimental woman who worked at the depot: "Don't trouble yourself to contact me; it is enough to thank me in your prayers and to pass the favour along sometime to someone else. Signed – *A Friend in the Lord*."

There'd been the Caribbean, an "all-seniors tour" (meaning, if you had the time and money to go you were old enough to suit the operators) with Happy Jack Bumpter and his third wife Lilluth, presumably *Lillus*, for Happy Jack had a pronounced lisp.

For Ulla's part, she was determinedly unpartnered at the time and so she had opted for having Lilluth/Lillus choose her a "share-mate" from the other singles who had signed up. And she'd got Bridget O'Brien (to this day she could not believe the name) who was as beautiful a woman as was ever a colleen of song or story. This Bridget, at the age of fifty-three, was as unlined of face and as shapely of figure as a cancan dancer. She was cherry-cheeked and round-faced, wide-eyed and ingenuous-looking. She tippled all day on the bus from an old vanilla bottle of gin, replenishing the bottle each night. It didn't take all night to do that, so she spent the rest of it castigating Ulla as "a typical WASP, high-handed as a lord, just like all the English".

"I haven't an English bone in my body," Ulla had said, at the first haranguing. "I'm Canadian. German genes as far back as you can go." Then, "Well, you never know, maybe a few Irish seeds way back there somewhere in the fourth century." Sometimes if you jollied people along you could brush these little chips off the shoulder at the start and get on with things.

But Bridget was not to be jollied. She had tippled and scolded, and tippled and scolded, and it had been about the longest three weeks of Ulla's life.

Hawaii. England. Scotland, Australia. Zimbabwe, for heaven's sake! At the behest of the nagging hassler just behind the left eye she had stirred her lazy bones to resolution and made plans and found the money. She had gone; she had seen; she had conquered – at least *quelled* – the desperate urge to book passage home the third day away each and every time.

Why should it be different this time? The ancestral home thing had never been a need of hers, not even a temporary interest as had England, for example, or the life-in-a-vanilla-bottle Caribbean. For them to come to pass it had been simply a matter of discipline – to decide to root the self from the safe haven of the little home at the edge of bush country in what passed for "northern Saskatchewan" in the minds of those who lived south of Prince Albert and Tisdale and North Battleford.

"I have a sister," members of her own family would say (sometimes it was "I have an old auntie" – with emphasis, Ulla suspected, on the *old*). "She lives in a little log house – yes, I said *log* house – and studies psychology and philosophy from out-of-date books, and cuts her own wood (and keeps the house so cold in winter you have to drink tea at her kitchen table wearing gloves and a parka – and at that, you'd better drink fast or it'll freeze cup to lip, I kid you not!)."

She'd heard that one at a wedding, standing quietly behind the large back of a favourite nephew, with a tray of glasses filled to the brim, in the prodigal manner of the bride's father, with good red wine. One often heard such remarks, having been damned by nature to prefer being the quiet observer, the one who faded into the background everywhere as though the magic cloak of invisibility, longed for so earnestly as a child, was now a mantle-constant about the shoulders.

All her life she had heard people talk about "going home". As a child, the first time or two, she was glad to hear it for she supposed it meant the company would be up and off and away from the table leaving a jelly doughnut or so still on the plate – which she meant to snap up as soon as her mother marshalled the guests to the door. Later, she found out it meant they wanted to *leave* home – leave a snug house and the pine trees and the whiskey-jacks and the summer of green growing things and the autumn of yellow-gold harvest. To go to a *foreign* land. A land they called *home* for some unexplained reason.

She had learned long ago it was useless to try to get an explanation from her mother. From her mother it was always, "If you have time to stand here talking I suppose that means you have finished weeding the turnips, have you?" So when she *was* finished with the turnips she would hike on over to Uncle Wilfred's little house, the one that was to be hers one day, and where there were never any turnips to need weeding.

Uncle Wilfred used to claim it was mostly the English who talked about "going home". "They can't help it," he said, "they've been conditioned all their lives to see Canada as the Colonies and themselves as cultural pioneers who are helping to civilize the place before they get reprieved and called back home."

Ulla had not bought the argument even at fifteen, sitting in the sole "guest-chair" in the small log house and discussing, or, more likely, listening to a discourse from Uncle Wilfred regarding many things not necessarily set out in the pages of the books he prized so. She had often been at the homes of school-mates whose parents, especially the mothers, spoke of home as being across the seas in Poland or Romania or the Ukraine (or, yes, Bavaria or Swabia or Schwartzwald). In her own family, home was *home*, as in: When I told you to get home right after school I *didn't* mean go right to Uncle Wilfred's, and you know it!

In later years, speculating alone and late at night, now sitting in Uncle Wilfred's chair, it had come to her that her parents had had some sort of unspoken agreement, a discipline of a peculiar kind to burn one's bridges to the old land and old ways completely and so make the life in Canada not only more bearable, but that which is preferred. They had been peaceful folk, her parents, and how can there be peace if words are forever chewing over another landscape, another way of doing things, another way of saying things than all that surrounds one in the new but chosen place one lives.

Once she had been fond of talking. Once, nursing the hot black tea in the big metal CPR mug that was the prerogative for the one occupying the guest-chair, willing Uncle Wilfred to leave the kitchen long enough so that she could add a little hot water to the strong brew he was so proud of offering, she had forgotten herself so much as to offer, "But Uncle Wilfred, consider this: on both sides of the family the people who will not speak of Germany as home or even speak the language in their own kitchens still give their children the old names – Ulla, Wilfred, Karl, Wilhelm, Irmgard, and on and on. They're hanging on to *something*, surely, when they do that, because who in his right mind would call a new baby Adolph at a time when anything hinting of . . . you know, all that . . . is better left undone?"

"True," said Uncle Wilfred. And that is where he had left it. He had risen from the high Captain's chair he had made himself from spruce cut a few feet from his cabin, the chair's dimensions to suit his small frame, its wide wings to shelter . . . what? *His* need for invisibility? He had gone into the tiny room that served him as bedroom and study, to look up a point in one of the books from the shelves that lined the four walls from floor to ceiling wherever possible. She had seized the moment to dilute the wicked swamp water he called tea and to begin her introduction to Jung, one she recognized as an inner master before she had completed the first chapter.

An hour later Uncle Wilfred returned, shame-faced. "I found an interesting point, I'm afraid, to support a contention I've been searching confirmation for for a long time now, and I have, therefore, forgive me, my dear, forgotten what was the issue between us. Will you refresh my memory?"

She didn't want to. Didn't need to, somehow. It was as though it didn't matter enough. She did not want to remove herself from the sunlit windows of Jung's darkness (those were the pictures she saw in her mind as soon as she began to read) even long enough to beg leave to borrow the book, and she was planning already to harbour herself within a very few minutes of her departure in an alcove of the aspen bush just down the lane to re-enter that adventure-of-mind Jung was setting out so clearly for those too young to be afraid.

Unafraid. True, she announced to herself, perhaps with a modicum of pride, she had always been unafraid. Lazy. That too. Let us say too contented, perhaps. Too unadventurous, as a matter of course, but surely, even serenely, unafraid.

But that, of course, was a different matter. The point of interest to her analytical mind just now was this: Why should someone who seemed to have so little conditioning "to be German" in her psychologicial make-up, be so taken with a land she had never really wanted to see?

Yet here she was now, ensconced cozily on the roof-storey balcony of an oldish six-floor apartment house in a small university city in the Black Forest, purportedly beginning to write her memoirs for a persuasive nephew to whom she had never learned to say No, but actually doing little more than take into mind and heart – and, almost incidentally, into the body – the South German sun of late May. Here she was now, looking off into the hills to the mistily blue-green of the ordered Wald where, once Walter and Christabel had gone to work, she walked now daily, footsteps soft upon the carpet of innumerable years of fallen leaves and needles, hearing no sound save the singing of birds until, as she climbed higher and higher, she began hearing, too, the silent words of mind saying: *I've come home.*

She did not need a compass to walk into the forest here. At home, in the bush country of Saskatchewan, she had not dared to venture far without one. Four hundred feet into the dank undergrowth and closely-knit spruce on a cloudy day and her head was a-buzz with that "Where in God's name am I?" feeling of occupying two worlds at one time, both of them unfamiliar. Here she walked eagerly on well-trodden paths, almost as though she was a wise old doe and this her carefully considered place.

Perhaps it had to do with the genes, after all, Walter had speculated in his careful, precise English. Given the fact that her maternal grandmother's family name had been traced back over three hundred years in this very region, might there not conceivably be the patterns of some ancient woodsman ancestor reporting through her particular genetic code?

"Always with you it's the complicated," Christabel had insisted, pouring more red wine. "It's just one of those things. In München I never get lost; in Stuttgart I am . . . how does one say it? . . . *wie ein Kind* . . . yes, as a little lost child. In Venice too. But put me in Paris and I can find for you the little pension of Mme Lafleur from any part of the city. It's just one of those things."

It was nearly ten o'clock at night. The sky still held the colours of sunset, but in delicate pastels. In the branches of a tremendous *Platane* (at home she would have guessed maple) a black bird homely as a starling sang so melodiously and so persistently it might have been the soundtrack for a nature video.

They were eating out. Some *schwäbisch* dish that reminded Ulla very much of wonton soup in the Golden Dragon at home. Outside tables. The second floor balcony of a four-hundred-year-old house four hundred yards from a castle eight hundred years old which tourists visited eagerly and then drove down to the town's centre with its decorative market square and its deliberately antiquated shops and restaurants, unaware that they had spun by this invincible eatery where the owner-chef did his best to appease at small expense to the pocketbook the hunger of young men and women who had sought out, from all over the world, the university (and then, by extension, the Swabian cooking) here.

"Walter didn't want to come here tonight," Christabel laughed, resting one hand briefly on his sweatered arm. "He is at cross-purposes with all that smacks of Schwaben just now."

Walter looked guilty. "Not really," he said.

"Yes, really," Christabel insisted. "We are having difficulties with our *schwäbisch* landlord just now. He will not fix the plumbing. He insists on greater rent. He . . ."

" . . . is entirely living up to the meaning of his name, the cockroach," grumbled Walter.

"*Schwabe* means cockroach," Christabel said. "It is a bad joke. One ought not to make it, but we do. We have our conditionings, too, you know. We want to be such perfect people now, this generation after the war, but somehow we get caught up in our little likes and dislikes, just like anyone else."

"It's a little thing," said Ulla. "Harmless." She wondered if it *was* harmless. It was, perhaps, a little like saying "our Natives" or "our Ukrainians" at home in Saskatchewan. Patronizing, in a way.

"There are no little things anymore," Christabel said.

"Not with her, at least," Walter grinned. "The whales, the seals, the guest workers here in Germany, the holy spirit, unification, her mother's birthday: everything, everything is one big deal with this one." He knuckled her shoulder. "Right?"

The town clock struck the hour – first, at Fa on the scale, the four strokes that indicated a tolling of the full hour was coming up; then, at Do-below-Re, the actual strokes of the hour. One automatically sang the pattern and counted the sounds on the Inner, inside the head where certain sounds played more surely than via the ears, waiting for the strokes of the Lutheran Church next, at the edge of the Wald, to cut in with its version half-way through the countdown.

The waiter hovered. They had been there a long time, even by the standards of university students. Ulla admired his German and Walter said, "It isn't real; he has learned it in Switzerland" (he said *Swisserland*; it sounded quite charming) "and his mother tongue is English."

"You have met him before," Ulla said.

"No, no," said Christabel. "He is new. Walter can tell these things."

Ulla checked. The young man was an American and the rest was as Walter had said. True enough, he was new, for he'd had trouble keeping his thumbs out of the soup. He wore a simple silver ring in one ear and was "blond from a bottle" in Walter's estimation.

There were few people left at the tables, on either the higher or lower balconies, and the few bits of conversation that drifted up to them were in German and had to do with the day-to-day affairs of the speakers. Christabel whistled cigarette smoke softly away from the table. Walter looked off toward the hills and was silent.

"Walter sits again in a dream world," said Christabel. "He is just lately back in Germany, as I've earlier told you."

Walter turned to them. "I'm here," he said.

"You were in Zimbabwe again," she challenged, smiling.

He looked a bit sheepish. "No, I don't think so. But I would go back there in a minute if I did not have a three-year contract with my firm. At thirty-five one must begin to be stalwart about some sort of career plan."

"*Teaching* is a career," said Christabel. Ulla got the notion this was ground that had been covered over and over before.

"Teaching German to the young in Zimbabwe has its satisfactions and its merits," said Walter, "but it drains the energy too much after too many years."

"Then teach here."

"You know why not. I will not be told by the system where I must teach: *Stuttgart needs a teacher of the Sciences; you go there*! *Ah, but if you please, sir, I do not care for the atmosphere in such an industrialized place. Tough! we need you, you go there, or you quit!* That's not for me anymore, that kind of mentality." His voice was calm, the words were precisely articulated.

"Watch his eyes," said Christabel. "Whenever he speaks like that, watch his eyes. When they shoot sparks, prepare to run, Ulla – he is one of the revolutionaries: a socialist turned individualistisch." She tapped his wrist with the hand that held the ever-present cigarette. He waved its smoke off with the other hand, laughed, signalled the waiter for the bill.

"No, seriously, Cousin," he said to Ulla, "by us things go too well; *too* well! One becomes lazy in the heart all the while the body and mind are working, producing, working, producing." He tapped his breast for emphasis. "Lazy in the heart," he said, and shook his head.

"I don't see it that way," Ulla said. "The East Germans come by the thousands and are welcomed; the immigrants pour in from Poland and Turkey and goodness knows where else and everyone says: 'Make them welcome! Make them welcome!' I hear it everywhere."

"Let us go now," said Christabel.

Walter ignored her. "Oh yes," he said to Ulla. "For public consumption they say it. As you were saying the other night is happening in Canada now. Welcome for public consumption. I don't know how it will be for your country but I know within myself that here, twenty years from now, there will be ghettos where the 'new Germans' have been encouraged to settle so that they can be 'comfortable' with their own language, their own customs. You will see!" His voice was rising.

"I can't even see the point of this discussion," said Ulla. "What is the subject and how did we drift into it? We were discussing the waiter's hair, the last I remember."

Christabel had been standing with her hand on Walter's shoulder, applying pressure with it now and again as a reminder for him to leave. Now she sat down again. "It's just the way it is for us now," she said, lighting another thin smoke. "So many our age are forever alert to mistakes, to errors – our own or our elders' or our politicians' – mistakes that will bring us again into disrepute. We want a perfect Germany, the most of us: well-ordered, efficient, kindly, colourful . . ."

" . . . *praiseworthy!*" Walter added, with the twist of an upper lip.

"Very well then, yes: praiseworthy," said Christabel.

"Moral!" offered Walter, arising from his chair.

"Moral, yes. And welcoming and blooming and productive. That's enough for anyone. Let's go."

"No! *Aware!*" said Walter. He was standing half-way down the stone steps, handing Christabel down the last few steps to the street with one hand while guiding Ulla, on the higher steps, with the other. "If we do not live permanently and vigilantly *aware* . . ."

"*Enough*, I said!"

"All the same," said Ulla, taking the last word by virtue of whatever status would give it to her – age, house guest, friend – "it is a good land and I have met only good people here, and as far as I am concerned, I have found my heart's home."

The next day she was accosted by a young punk with pink spiked hair, a baby-pink complexion, and very bad teeth which he put to good use by baring them of thin painted lips in a wide grimace. She had been in an ancient church puzzling over the paintings of a local artist of the day who was patently from some post-modern school. She'd bent a casual conciliatory knee toward the main altar behind which Jesu suffered according to the oils (and inner images) of someone who might well be emulated, in Ulla's uneducated opinion, by the young artist of the foyer exhibition. Then, since she seemed to be utterly alone in the church she slipped under a thin gold rope and skipped quickly up the slender marble spiral staircase to the high priest's podium to make a quick inspection from that vantage point (and feeling, for the moment it took, a little like the pater of a flock in ancient times).

She had to duck out of sight when someone came in. She held her breath, but in short order heard their steps recede, echoing, echoing, and so she let her bad right knee scold her for her foolishness and made her way down and out in nothing flat.

There was a *Bäckerei* nearby and she allowed herself to be seduced by the fragrance of baked sesame seed and good oil and cinnamon and cardamom and fine white sugar. She was happily munching a *Rosinen Schnecke*, trying to analyze whether it was the aroma or the taste that delighted her more, and walking where her body took her.

All at once it stopped, simply stopped. And something inside her said: *No, not this way*! But she made a quick decision and went anyway down the dark steps to the narrow side street she had not noticed before.

He came out of nowhere, raced towards Ulla. He was with a young woman taller than himself and they were laughing. The girl said something challenging to him in a language Ulla did not understand and the ugly youth broke away from her, sprinted to Ulla's side, held out his hand and rasped, "*Funf Mark, bitte! Funf Mark, bitte!*"

Ulla was so astounded she almost stopped in her tracks to try to find out what this was all about. But something inside her said: *Keep walking!* Her mind turned to soup then and she could not even find any words to use, so she just kept walking and saying only, "*Bitte! Bitte!*"

The young man kept pace with her, grabbed her shoulder, stuck his face close to hers. "You're not German, you ugly old bitch!" he said. "Give me money, freak!"

The blood had turned to glue in her veins. The pressure of his hand went through her like a knife; she was as sure as sure that he had already stuck her with a blade.

He pulled her to a stop, placed the hand that had been cupped and supplicating now flat on her chest. The two hands of him applied pressure, his face full of homely teeth and his sharp zip-dancing eyes too close, too close, to her own.

"*Money*, stupid bitch!" he said. Said it quite calmly, punctuating the words with the pressure of that hand on her chest. Could he detect the small canvas money sack under her coveralls? Was this the way it was to be afraid? "*Bitte!*" she pleaded, hating herself for giving in to fear. He was shoving her now, moving her towards the darker shadows under the steps.

Her body stopped of its own accord. With one twist of the body she had broken loose, but she did not run. "*Geh schon weg!* you little fucker," she hissed, "*ob's kommt Polizei und* Canadian consulate and I don't mean maybe!"

She turned her back on him and walked briskly towards the light of the wider street. She did not know where the tall young woman was now and she did not mean to look. Perhaps she ran the last few steps. Later, she couldn't remember, but most of the tender warm *Rosinen Schnecke* had been converted to a dampish unpalatable lump in one clenched fist. For some reason she kept it there until she was crossing one of the city's several small rivers. Standing in the sunlight she fed it to the ducks.

For the next three days she walked only in the woods or in the neighbourhood immediate to Christabel and Walter's flat. Each day she bought the supper rolls from the same small *Bäckerei*, the vegetables from a small place that advertised itself as a flower shop but kept open trays of the basics – potatoes, onions, cabbage and the like – here and there amongst the potted geraniums and cut flowers.

The shop was so small you had to stand in line to enter, while the tiny bell announcing customers seemed utterly superfluous since the same large white-haired woman in a flowered smock sat the entire working day, it seemed, behind the counter, stretching one arm to the left for potatoes to weigh on the small table scale before her, the other arm to the right for onions or tulips. A little farther to the right and she got you salt or *Zwieback*. Whenever there was something she could not reach she leaned back on her stool, took a great breath of air, and her loud summons brought a slight, pale Her-MANN! to you in no time at all.

When Walter and Christabel came home from the one hour's commute from the industrial smoke and commercial efficiency of Stuttgart, she had ready some dish her mother had served as standard fare when Ulla was young – potato dumplings, perhaps, with the *Rotwurst* and fried onions Walter fancied, and a cheap good Tyrol wine.

Walter was going back to Zimbabwe. He had had an argument with his chief at the magazine he worked for about toeing the American line. "We're a subsidiary here, you must remember," the chief had said. "These things are decided before they ever reach this department. It's just a matter of formality."

"But we *voted* on the issue! Why did we bother to vote on the issue if there was no possibility of taking an opposing view to that of the parent company? It's so crazy! Why did we vote?"

"It's just a matter of formality," said the chief. "It's the way things are done."

The way Walter did things was to clear out his desk then and there and then make one phone call. From a public pay phone. By next week he would be gone.

"Are you going, too?" Ulla asked Christabel, and wished the minute the words were out that she had not.

"Of course not," said Christabel. "It is Walter's thing." But later she said, "Don't you be sad, my new friend. For me. For him. He will be back in two years' time."

"I don't know about that," said Ulla. "He has a very *un*lazy heart, that one."

"True enough," said Christabel, lighting another cigarette, "but unlazy heart or not, what German in his right mind would ever decide to call Zimbabwe *home*?"

It had been hot in the flat from all the cooking. But now it was ten o'clock and cooler. One of the black ugly starlings was whistling and yodelling twenty different songs at once through the open window. The starling had a name handsomer than its physiognomy: *Amsell.* Blackbird.

The city clock began its spiel. “In the meantime,” said Christabel, “you will stop here and be my suite-mate, won’t you, Ulla? It would be so nice.”

The time had not presented itself to tell the others there had been a call earlier from Canada. Someone wanted to buy Ulla’s place. Uncle Wilfred’s place. It was said they were enchanted with the old log house and they did not believe in changing things too much. They were a pair who had committed themselves, they said, in a sacred vow, to never cut down a living tree.

At home, Ulla thought now, at ten o’clock at night no birds would be singing. No sooner had she thought the thought when, as though at some given signal, the blackbird broke off its baroque, its captivating song.

ALLES VERRÜCKT

He seemed to be inside a loud wide box. He could see out, but out was as unfamiliar as in. *Es war alles verrückt*, the whole thing was crazy. Before him a creature clinging with clenched claws to a round apparatus – a wheel? – snarled something seemingly addressed to Martin himself.

Martin looked quickly about. There were other beings in the box, all of them looking only at him. He looked down to shut them out, saw his own hands, remembered then about hands, smiled at the magic of them, clenched and unclenched them, looked then to the being who clenched a wheel in his hands, knew then the being had been roaring, looking, pointing at Martin himself.

Somehow, he knew he was Martin for now – only for now; there was a knowingness within him that it was but a temporary measure. And with that knowingness came another: Martin had a devil, one who could be trusted to translate the miasmic roaring that spewed from the . . . what? . . . oh yes, the *mouths*, the mouths of creature beings.

Martin's devil spoke. *He is telling you to put one Mark in the coin box. The coin box is before you. The coin is for passage. There is a coin for this purpose in the right-hand pocket of your trousers. Don't do it. Put nothing in the coin box. This hard impatient creature detests the company that gives him livelihood; he will signal you to sit and you will ride for free.*

Martin's angel spoke. Whenever he had to be this Martin, there was this angel that came along too. Too vaguely, too mistily, too softly, so that often he could not see or hear or understand her – unlike Yousaf, his devil, who walked beside him, black and fulsome, whenever he chose to, and who shouted unsolicited advice into his mind.

But now it was the angel spoke. *Martin, dear love, in your pocket* – in die Tasche – *ready to hand, lie two coins. Can you find them? feel them with your fingers? Good. Ah, so. Now, separate them, there's a dear, and bring forth one.* He did so. *Good.* Gut. *Now place it in the coin box.* He did so, enjoyed the tinkling clatter as it disappeared; felt distress, for some reason too, at the disappearance. *Good boy. Good fellow . . . oh but you Germans do give one a time of it sometimes . . . now sit. Sit! No, no, no, not on the floorboards,* nicht um Fusboden . . . *you are a man, a human; sit as these others are sitting. See? Yes,* ja ja ja, das ist richtig, *that's a dear.*

A world passed by. Some sort of world passed by. One could see out of the box, a box which moved, and then stopped, and then moved and stopped and moved and stopped again, all very quickly and with no fluid flow or harmony whatsoever. At one of the stops Martin's devil said, "To hell with this!" aloud, using Martin's mouth to say it. Then he spilled his blackness off the lap of a large dour creature of ample belly sitting across from Martin, floated out of the box and was gone.

Besides the large one nearby there were many creatures, beings. There was much noise. Nothing was a melody and Martin, though he tried, could discipline no harmony out of it, only *Lärm, Lärm, Lärm*; soon there would be fires all about, no doubt, and the . . . the things called . . . the loud things called . . .

Bombs, said Martin's angel. *The name your mind is looking for is the name called bombs. The bombs are over, Martin. A while ago. You are an old man now. Man! Remember about men? See the stick you carry? Yes, yes, the stick. Tap it three times on the floor . . . dear, dear,* Fusboden, *then . . . three times, so that I will know you understand. Three times. Yes, good. Listen: there are no more bombs. Have you got that? No more bombs.*

A sudden and terrible angst filled Martin's body. In his heart and head there was a pounding; under the armpits, in the fingertips, in the toes there was a pounding. He had all the words for it; he had them in German and he had them in English and in French and Spanish, too, if the dark people with cold weapons made him talk again. He had the words for: *If there are no more bombs, where am I now and what is the new danger?*

He spoke the words aloud then. "Where am I now and what is the new danger?" He looked about, peering towards corners, trying to assess – to sniff out, if necessary – the danger.

A young lithe one, sitting nearby, turned as if to speak to him. He had the words for her: girl, not yet young woman; *Mädchen. Mädchen* felt better. Two sorts of words for her were enough. He had the words, too, for her intentions, for he read them in the air, without looking at her, looking now only at his stick and at the floorboards.

"Don't speak to him," said someone, a large female someone sitting beside the young one. "*Immer alles verrückt*, with that one. Crazy, crazy; don't answer him; once you answer him you will have him on your hands; once you answer him he talks and talks – gets off where you do and follows you and talks and talks and talks."

Once you answer him he talks and talks. Once you answer him he talks and talks. *And that is you, Martin, they are talking about. You.* Said the angel. *Sit still.* Said the angel. *We are not there yet.*

It was a bus. Yes, of course; it had come to him now, he was on a bus. They were on a bus. It stopped. Too quickly. Martin fell to the side. He righted himself, groping for the three shopping bags, two white, one gold, he had with him always when he was Martin. There should be a stick too. Was there one today? He asked the angel.

You threw it at a dog, said the angel. *Sit still.*

No, said Martin. *There was a stick, for I tapped it three times for you. Three times. I don't know why I had to do it but I can read it in the air now: I tapped the stick.*

Good boy! said the angel. *Now sit still.*

"You get off here!" The man who held the wheel of the bus in his hands roared it the next time, "YOU GET OFF HERE."

Martin looked about him. He counted his bags, one, two, three, and looked about him.

"YOU!" said the man. He pointed a fist at Martin. Or maybe at his angel. Martin looked over his shoulder to see if he could see the angel today, in hopes he could see the angel today. She was still there and just now she was bright and she was shining. "You get off here, *Dummkopf*, I said!"

Martin stood up. He counted his three shopping bags again and shuffled about, adjusting his cap, his gloves, trying to button the buttonless coat. Somewhere there was a stick. If his devil would but arrive he would soon have that stick.

The woman – he had seen her many times before, he knew that, just now – the one who had kept the younger one in her seat when she meant to speak to him, now half-rose and leaned towards the driver. "He doesn't get off until Rosenkranzestrasse and you know it! You let him be!"

The door of the bus hissed shut with a final slam. The bus started up again. Martin fell into an empty seat. He counted his shopping bags and then sat firm, watching out the window.

There is no more danger, said the angel from the seat directly behind him. *You have passed the test and I have found your stick.* Sure enough, the stick appeared, foot first, over his right shoulder, from behind him. *I have read the day*, said the angel, *and we shall walk together and remember it well for we have just passed another test, together.*

I have had it to the breast bone with these tests, Martin told her, but sat, knowing that he must trust.

One block before they came to the park, just after they passed the SparKasse with its large bright glowing red letters reminding him always of red candy canes in the stockings at Christmas in some lifetime when there had been few dangers about, the square box SparKasse with the white papers in the window telling the passerby what gold was worth today, he pressed the red STOP button on the shiny steel post before him. He used to try to see himself in the bright surface when he was younger, but it had made him ill, staring at his disfigured visage, so now he simply concentrated on the red button to make sure the bus would stop. Once, before he had discovered one must do so, the bus had overshot the stop and he'd had to walk back six blocks, so now he concentrated fiercely on the dull red circlet to enforce his wishes upon the bus.

Once it had come to a full stop he rose, counted his shopping bags once again, made his way carefully to the door, then just as carefully dismounted by way of three steps to the sidewalk.

Then he was safe. He sighed deeply; he took stock of his bags again, then began to make his way over the green green grass, admiring it and the dew still in the clover in it on his way to the duck pond.

He had hardly settled himself on the short red bench on the sun's side of the pond when they came fluttering and flapping towards him across the surface of the lake.

May you live in grace, Herr Oswald, said the largest drake, if you have brought us bread.

I shall live in grace, and so shall you, said *der grosser Herr*, Herr Oswald, if you will ever learn to make way first for your smaller brothers and sisters, at table!

The drake bowed and bowed then, first left, then right, then thrice directly towards his lord. Ah, but *Mein Herr*! You have bread and I have need of it. Give me, so that I may wax fat and strong to care for these, my brethren.

I shall sit here all day in the sun, giving nothing, and you know it, unless you move off and allow the smaller cousins their bread. He tightened his hold on the three bags, held them high, shook them at the feathered mandarin. I am Oswald, Graf von Hansemann, and I declare to you, the smallest shall be first fed!

He stood, clenched hand aloft, holding again the circular white-and-gold shield of his ancient house, challenging the sun, if necessary, for the people must be fed. The great drake bobbed, looked aloft; bobbed, looked aloft. Then it wheeled abruptly about, with no bending of the neck to his Herr, the Graf of Hansemann, and with a quick flick of the tail, moved off.

Herr Oswald took note of the stiff neck, the disrepectful tail flick. The smaller ones flocked forward immediately and he fed them carefully. Those who had some hindrance, and who stayed, therefore, always to the side and behind the stronger ones, their tired eyes darting here and there in hopes of a stray morsel, those he paid special attention to, speaking to them with the familiar *du*, and tongue-tsking kiss calls to them to bring them closer.

Because of the large drake's arrogance Oswald gave him the discipline of bobbing quietly for nearly half an hour in the shadows of a brooding *Kastanie*, its bottommost branches sheltering the green-growing bank, its shadows a threat and yet a harbour.

Then: Here, sir, is bread! he called, his deep sure voice carrying good cheer and great kindliness. He sent a handful of the good firm brown bread, carried always in the gold-coloured sack to be more easily told, now his eyes were failing, from the white stuff, poorer, but more readily available from the bakers' helpers who could get away with discarding the cheap white table rolls each day when he called – sometimes before the sun was up.

As soon as he sent the good bread sailing high into the air to fall before the great *Bürger* sulking in the shadows – to fall, as it were, as the manna once fell (at least, so it is written) for those others strong enough to command it from their lord – the rest of the flock turned and twittered, as though torn between two opportunities.

Stay, stay; *your* bread is here! With calm command Oswald brought them into comfort again. He fed them, heard their troubles, gave considered advice (but only when petitioned). All day he lived inside the heart of the sun, with this other green and blue and scarlet world of grass and trees and water and *Mohn* blooms somehow an extension of his true world inside the golden orb.

Within the heart of the sun his world was white and gold. There were no troubles there, no need for mediation, no loud sounds to cry out *Lärm! Lärm!* Here presents itself a new danger.

Within the heart of the sun, all wore crowns, the geese and ducks and camels too. It was an elegance; it was a gracing; it was a full-shining way to be.

But always, always, one was in some way committed to deal with a green and blue and scarlet world where disharmonious sound smashed the basic ions of man-made things, broke autobuses into the essentials of matter and rebuilt them as glassed and mobile traps that stank of the egestion of the sweat glands of creatures and the bowels of machines. Then one's comforting hold on the worlds within the heart of the sun became tenuous and there arose in the breast the black discomfort called fear, the danger that screamed one could lose one's grasp of the true reality and become lost in the green and blue and scarlet world forever.

When the sun was low across the lake he would gather up his bags and check his pockets for the wherewithal to take him elsewhere. During the day he, along with the drake, had eaten of the good solid brown-grain bread; water, the second staple, flowed constantly from a nearby fountain. Many times he had heard mothers cautioning children not to drink the water. Only water from a bottle was safe now, the mothers scolded; the television had said so.

And so it goes: in years gone by, mothers quoted chapter and verse from some bible in order to teach and scold, teach and scold; now they quoted the television. And just as in years gone by, the children went their own way anyway – drank the fountain's waters anyway, as the ducks tippled from the algaed pond – and most thrived to grow into fortune and misfortune as ever has been the way of ducks and of children.

If he stayed too long at his work – because there had been too many problems among the lesser folk, or because the great drake had been utterly and completely fractious – there were times when he felt himself becoming Martin again. Perhaps a pair of lusty young lads came by, pedalling bicycles and gobbling ice creams in a way to remind one of the energies and delights of a young body and sound innards, and they might call cheerfully to each other, "There's that crazy old fool again – *alles verrückt!* right?" Then he would feel himself becoming Martin again, and he would begin to count his white and gold plastic bags again – *eins, zwei, drei*; *eins, zwei, drei* – and almost at once his angel would be there or, sometimes, his devil.

If it was his angel she would be sure to say, *You are Martin if you wish it so. In the right-hand pocket of your trousers lie the coins to take you aboard the bus. It is your choice. But, if you will come walk with me, will lift high your feet in regard for the uneven cobblestones, will hold your head and your shoulders erect because you are one of the chosen ones – and if you will speak only to me, listen only to me – I shall take you safely home.*

Most often they would walk. If there were three coins in his pocket they would buy bread early tomorrow at the back doors of the bakeshops. At the angel's behest he would search the bottom of the gold bag for crumbs and snippets of the good brown bread and allow each portion to be masticated thoroughly and deliciously in his mouth for the count of two hundred steps, its flavours enhanced by the practice, its aromas set forth so and stealing into nasal passages and brain, a heightened experience that never failed to raise before his eyes the very fields that had grown good brown *Korn* – wheat and oats and maize and barley – on his grandfather's farms at the edge of the Pfalzer Wald so long, so long ago.

He had not needed the worlds within the heart of the sun in those times. He had been golden content with forest and fields and with harmonious white water busily making its way to his uncle's mill where his uncle's miller ground his grandfather's grain into the meal that made the good hot brown bread that graced mid-table for every meal set by his grandmother's cook – supervised closely always by her Lady – on the sturdy table in the large kitchen because the Lord willed to eat not amidst the polish and gilt of the great cold dining room where (so it was often told) kings with their queens (or, sometimes, their mistresses) had been in earlier times plied with red wine and fed on good *Pfalzer* hare and bread and beef.

In those times he had known always who he was. In those times he had lived richly among the scarlet poppies of summer and waxed free and content. Even then his angel was there, although then he could not see her; rather, he knew her presence through the needle-sharp specklings of a cold- and hot-running electricity that coursed over the entire surface of his body; he knew her through a certain special fragrance, the perfume of flowers not of this world; he knew her through the voice that spoke, sun-coloured and blue-fluid and melodious, inside his head.

In those times he had no need of her, and yet she came, with casual good cheer, to fly with him through the green meadows sprinkled with scarlet poppies and heady with the fragrance of clover in subtle bloom.

In those times, when the church bells rang to summon all believers, the angel spoke, less casually, to say he was free to go there, and free also to stay in the meadows or along the white-running brook. Sometimes he went along to the church with the others; sometimes he stayed in the world of young green and blue and scarlet: always, he was happy.

The day his grandfather died, he obeyed the summons of the bells and took unto himself the land and its people and their few joys and many sorrows. The day his uncle died he added the mill and the village workers.

Then came loud *Lärmen*, and unheard of dangers from the heavens, and he became Martin.

Martin! It was his angel, dressed in gold-white light. She had no face, no wings, no form other than the hot gold-white light of all-glory. Never before had he seen her so clearly. On the cold red asphalt of the green park's path, he knelt.

I have never believed in a God, he said, *but surely I am now in His presence!*

Ach, Gott ick seg! the angel replied, her voice the sound of perfected exasperation, *get up off your knees and let us proceed without nonsense, for this is the time I have chosen to enter the heart of the sun forever.*

YOU have chosen? demanded Herr Oswald, rising. *YOU have chosen? Be aware that I . . . I, have chosen to give bread to those who need me.*

I have chosen to accept you, said the angel, *and it is time, so, as for what YOU want: it just doesn't matter,* mein Kleiner, was du willst. Komm mit mir; mach' schnell, mach' schnell! es ist schon Zeit! She beckoned; her hands invited, pleaded.

He stepped off the cold red paved way and walked with sturdy step toward the brook where the water ran clean into the algaed lake; where the grass grew high, devoid of the scarlet flame of the poppy. Here he placed carefully the three bread sacks, the gold one for his head, the two white ones for his body. He positioned them precisely and smoothed them into place, his hands strong, steady.

Then he laid his body down and said to his angel, *I am ready.*

And then he was within the heart of the sun.

And then he was
that
golden
glowing
heart.

EMBODIED

If he'd come in from Venus, he'd have had a better time of it. There was all that "make love" stuff of the sixties; he could have melded with that then. And nowadays there was all this folderol of the so-called New Age. Same thing. Love. Vibrations. Go with the flow. Meld. As if it was easy. As if they really knew what it is all about. But if he'd come in from Venus it would have been easy. That was principle. But he'd come in from Iguano, worse luck, and it had been a barrel of crapola from start to finish.

Iguano. The story of his life: a cross between a dim-witted lizard and the piled up rock lime of half a million sea birds. Nothing else would do: *he* had to be of Iguanoan stock – efficient, faultlessly programmed, utterly feelingless.

It was an interesting state, to be sure. It could be analyzed and even appreciated, in the muted, ineffable way of mind. But to say the appreciation could be *felt* – a dancing near the heart, the spitter-spatter of sun specks throughout the veins, a tickling smile spreading in steady progression over the entire surface of the skin – would be presenting that-which-is-not-so, and no true Iguanoan would descend to such a practice, even to gain immediate passage home.

Home. Until he was sixty he had no memory of it. Well, that is to say, no true memory. Only dreams. Easy to call a dream a dream and let it go at that. In this primitive place words are the cop-out for everything.

* * * *

When I came in, the body was twelve Earth years old. A rather precocious twelve, it seems, if that is the appropriate word, for there had been, apparently, shortly before my entry, an episode in a shadowed poplar grove with a mature young lady of rich desires and happy availability. Whereupon the dark Calvinistic mind of the youth I had chosen to inhabit hounded him so ferociously he betook himself to the river and threw himself off a cliff in the general direction of what is still locally known as Broken Head Rock. With the hope of ending his shame forever.

It did. But hardly in the way he had intended. He missed the rock completely, but believed so utterly in his demise that his personality essence accepted the message and simply flew off to do its thing in "other realms", to put it delicately. And falsely. All those "other realms" are very much present in the here and now. And when the young fellow had learned his lessons and wanted the body back there was hell to pay, I can assure you, for by then I had agreed to attempt the earthly experiment and was lodged solidly (or as solidly as a personality of Iguanoan essence can be said to be lodged) within the body spewing water from its mouth at the behest of a passing farm hired hand and coughing a little blood into the bargain.

I do not mean to record here the events surrounding the attempts of Jason Everest to reclaim the body. This epistle will be difficult enough to set down, as it is. (And, as a matter of course, for most – particularly those once my fellows in the field of science – difficult in the extreme to digest.)

It is not my intention to be cavalier about it; the truth is, I bade the personality Jason Everest a civil adieu, having processed into his essence the information that he had chosen to leave this planet at the slightest challenge and therefore he was committed to a new beginning – for which, I suggested, he might well program himself with a bit more backbone and a modicum of man-made guilt. I have read the mind-essence records prior to setting about recording this experience and it is clear he was informed regarding the principle involved. So that is that.

For a short while after entering I remembered who I was and why I had come. As an Iguanoan of the 31st rank, having explored lives on thirty other planets, I was one committed now – by very virtue of the principle of progression – to the cruellest experiment: life in a stolidly material body amongst a race of beings ruled by feelings – their own, and the feelings of others.

My parents – one ought to say, for the present, *his* parents, I suppose – were dismayed, they said, to see their son in such sodden disarray as that in which the hired man presented me at the door of the Everest farm kitchen. When they heard his story – the story of their son's "swimming accident" – they were aghast, they said. Further, they were grateful and overjoyed, they said, to have him returned safe and hale – beyond an unsuitable pallor, they said – and relatively hearty. They thanked the Good Lord, they said; they thanked Wilbur, the hired man, they said. They did so most profusely, and insisted he stay for supper. They used a lot of words for all this, more to telephone Wilbur's employers to beg his absence from the evening chores, and eminently more, I suspect, during the course of the evening, while I – as Jason – was trundled, wordless, off to a warm bed with a hot water bottle to the feet and another at the heart region.

Years later it would be the mind's replay of those two blood-heat water bottles that would spark the entire computer program back into life. It allowed me, then, to remember: there was a brief time, when first I entered the body, that I could, in that peculiar way of humans, *feel.*

I do not mean *feel* in the sensory way; after all, there are many planets that have evolved a living body of sorts, and some of them have developed not five bodily senses, as has the race upon Earth, but seven. Language is such an awkward tool at the best of times and English one of the crudest. One must define terms over and over. I speak here, of course, of the aspect of *psychological* feeling: *inner* feeling, if you like.

And that first night on this planet, with a state of almost glowing warmth coddling the feet and chest – and with the head a-buzz with the halo of protective and supportive energy called "holy-white" on Iguano – I drifted in and out of Jason Everest's body (which was fast becoming "my" body), and I underwent a series of feelings.

I had never experienced emotions before. Unless the state of utter awareness, of perpetual all-knowingness, may be said to be an emotion. Yet here, in my first hours in an earthly body, I was experiencing perhaps the entire gamut that the race called "human" had permitted, through lack of discipline, to evolve.

They were stored in the brain, of course, these phenomena. Or, more correctly, in that spontaneous interaction of brain and lower mind that is occasioned by the fact that they – at the current stage of the *spiritual* evolution of this rather backward race – remain connected by an intricate cobwebbing of electrical "circuitry" even after the Earth-developed personality has gone on to other planes. In the highest form of the genus, of course, the brain and the mind are two separate entities.

In any case, in the body so lately that of Jason Everest, a not-so-highly-evolved soul, I *felt*. Oh, how I *felt*! And I saw, of course, the inner screen pictures tied to them, the only surprise there being how faulty the process of inner seeing tends to be in a human. On Iguano – as in most other "places" in the several universes, according to my early teachers – the picture-making is patently clear (and even, one might say in Earth terms, radiantly charismatic).

So I was given to feel again Jason Everest's mother's arms about me, molding his cold wet body to her warmth. The coming together of the two body fields zapped myriad tiny tingles of energy onto the skin. These seemed to penetrate then, and to coalesce in two places: inside the head, and around the heart.

The sensation was somewhat that of the warmth of the pale blue Iguanoan sun which fluctuates not one degree off perfection for forty days and forty nights, the period decreed by our constitution as High Summer.

I felt again her soft hands stroking Jason Everest's face, brushing the wet tangled hair from the eyes and gently, so gently, pressing her lips to them – one, then the other, then again the first. "Mother!" cried a voice in the brain. And I accepted the programming and was at peace.

During the course of the night, interrupted by too-frequent tip-toeings in on the part of one or the other of the parents, I saw and heard and smelled and tasted the past of Jason Everest seep from the brain. Some I snatched back into the program I was building, some I permitted to float off into forever, some I simply buried in the far mind as the most expeditious way of dealing with a twelve-year-old Earthling's prodigious input.

The incident in the poplar grove with the nubile young woman was one I was tempted to keep, for the feeling was so . . . exquisite. But it was followed, hard upon, always by a feeling so black, so dense yet so sharp it clawed at the bowels and at the brain, and even at the pale blue Iguanoan sun that was basting the heart so efficiently. The mother, on one of her tip-toeings, tsk-tsk-tsked quietly to find the bottle flung from the bed. She refilled it with blue sun and replaced it over the young heart while she crooned, "Don't fret, my dear and lovely boy, tomorrow the world will be set to rights and all as it used to be."

I slept for three days, surfacing only to the body's need to void and to the positive aromas occasioned by smoothly warm thin foods the brain called soup and porridge and hot cocoa. By then the body was mine and I was the body's. Human senses were faculties of the most efficient type, it seemed. They presented the scent of roses drifting in at the open window, the song of an oriole riding the rose essence but knowing, somehow, to bypass the nose and enter at the ears instead. The smell of bacon frying, as diagnosed and labelled by the brain, was presented on the inner screen quite efficiently, for the five rashers curlicued and draped themselves about in such a way as to spell B A C O N as it sizzled and grew lean in the pan.

In the kitchen my mother greeted me with much evidence of what she repeatedly called *Joy*. She called to my father, taking a post-breakfast pipe outdoors – for she permitted no desecration in her house, she said, either by word or by deed – and he rushed in, his face furrowed and grey at first, then all of a rosy smile to see me up and about again.

"You had us worried, Lad!" he said.

"I never for a minute worried," said my mother. "I prayed and prayed, but I never worried."

"Of course not, of course not," said my father, directing a broad wink of the eye my way. (Knowing, man-to-man stuff, signalled the brain.) "Of course not," said my father. "That's why you were out of bed eighty-seven times every night checking on him: so you could 'not worry' more efficiently."

Then the words poured out, on and on from both of them, meeting often too close to the ears and brain and making me hold my head. Then there was food on a plate for me and more hot black coffee in a huge mug for my father. And my mother said, "Oh well, light up that smelly old Hades you call a pipe then; I'll open a window and let the roses in as soon as you take Jason off to school."

"I shall ride Jackie," I said, surprising myself.

"Of course you will; of course you will," my father agreed, between puffings of pipe smoke. There was something of the aromatics of an Iguanoan healing circle about that smoke, and for a flash I received the thought, and I heard the word *Iguanoan*. But then it was as though a hatch was slammed shut somewhere on a black metal box that both surrounded and yet permeated me. I had built for myself a solid protection to live life on Earth undetected. Everything I needed was there, boxed in in the computer program. So I became Jason Everest and knew not for nearly fifty years all else I was – and all else I was not.

For the rest of my years in a little country school I was frequently nonplussed by the actions of a classmate who smiled at me often from behind her books, who seemed to be wherever I went, who sang "Hell-OH, Jason!" twenty times a day out of a mouth like the bud of some twinned rose that grew, surely, in no garden upon Earth, so full, so red, so perfect was it. The clarity of one's mind became confounded. There was a sensation of something stirring in the head and in the vitals whenever she spoke my name. The movement inside would grow, take on a life of its own, propose departure from the body in order to seek its quietude within the rose. But always, just in time, the hatch would slam shut somewhere, and all was safe again within the enclosure that was me.

At home on the farm I worked with both my father and my mother. I suppose, in the light of what is called today "the totally democratic family" by those who speak – sometimes, as it seems, unendingly – on the subject, we were a "liberated" family group, for my father and I often did the washing-up of the dinner dishes (he stealing a quick puff in the porch-pantry in winter rather than make a pipe, as per agreement, outdoors). In the meantime my mother played the German composers on the pianoforte. Her ancestors had fought their

England's invasions from France since the time of recorded history, she was fond of saying, and she meant to decry everything and anything French to the end of her days, and if that was a sin either venial or mortal, so be it.

My father's "Englishness" had been watered down by three generations of disciplined neighbourliness on the Saskatchewan prairie. His people had set more ploughshares into virgin soil, my mother said, than perhaps any other prolific and productive family line; and my father would smile behind his huge mug of hot black coffee and not deny it.

My father's holdings were, therefore, extensive. When my allotment of chores was done to his satisfaction I was free to roam, and I did so – sometimes aboard Jackie, the sleek, tough, painted "Indian pony" who never miscued or misstepped; sometimes on foot, ambling wherever my feet took me. Always I studied the land, its plants, its creatures, making copious notes in small black hardcover "field books" I labelled *The Journals of Jason E. Everest*, and wherein I also sketched the clouds, the flora and fauna that came my way, and recorded the direction of the wind.

Always I looked for what was never there: any kind of lizard.

"*Ugh!* thank goodness there are none of those repulsive creatures hereabouts," said my mother. "What peculiar interests you do have, Jason, I *must* say!" The time I found one staring at me from a crevice in the dirt walls of the cellar at my grandmother's lake cottage I became mesmerized at once. I huddled down before it, the tendrils of my mind undulating towards it and just beginning to worm their way into its small benignity as I heard my grandmother call from the trap door entrance to the cellar, "Goodness gracious sakes, boy, you don't have to sprout the entire potato bin, just fetch up enough for supper, if you please."

"He's been that way since the accident," I heard my mother say. "He goes . . . well, off into other worlds, you might say, at the drop of a hat. So unlike our Jason. I'm afraid it quite worries me."

"It's to be expected," my grandmother said, her voice casual, with just an edge that had more to do with the tardiness of the potatoes than with my mother's concern, I expect. "He'll soon get over it."

"I wonder," my mother said. "I do worry. It's as though . . . as though . . . oh, this is silly, but it's as though he is somebody else, somehow, sometimes. When you kiss him, for example. There's no response. It's like kissing . . . well . . . *a box*. That's what it's like, it's like kissing a box."

"Then quit kissing, Elvira," my grandmother said. "The lad is growing up and it's time to stop that; it always embarrasses them, you know . . . Oh, finally! Here's the potatoes, and none too soon, boy, none too soon."

On my sixteenth birthday my father gave me "one of those lizard books you've been mooning for." My mother expressed instant and very vocal disapproval, but I, as soon as it was in my hands, felt a door open somewhere inside the middle of my head, just for a flash. I did not open the book. I knew I had to be alone when "it" happened, though I had no inkling what "it" was. I excused myself as soon as I decently could, having expressed thanks profusely and repeatedly in the way I had learned would please my parents, and hurried upstairs where I shut myself in my room.

The book fell open at the family *Iguanidae*. There was the Common Iguana looking at me eye to eye, wide mouth well open in the over-large head, the pointed scales along its back signalling . . . what? . . . for they seemed to be undulating, undulating, as I looked. The page was a colour plate. The Common Iguana was a dark olive-green, the precise hue of the winter parka I had worn for four years and refused to discard although the sleeves were inches too short and the zipper had given out trying to keep my growing frame within bounds.

My ears were ringing. About my head there was a motion and a sound such as the buzzing of bees circling, circling, waiting their turns to enter and deposit their sweet loads. From somewhere a message flashed: *Welcome home!* I translated it as: I have found my mission in life. And I went downstairs to so advise my parents.

It was a foregone conclusion that any son of my mother would go to university, though that was certainly not the norm for Saskatchewan farm youths of the time. My mother had had an ancestor of the maternal line who had been illiterate even as a mature woman who worked in the woollen mill by day and threw herself, nightly, at the foot of the cross at the local Sally Ann. Having a bit of the Welsh in her, she loved to sing, her favourite "singalong" being a hearty rouser that repeated itself endlessly and was, therefore, easily learned by rote:

> I am saved (I am saved)
> I am saved (I am saved)
> I am S-A-V-E-D!

Night after night she led those assembled to proclaim their new status with this song. Once, one of the equally illiterate and always hungry street people who came in for the nightly service because it was a prerequisite for the thin soup and heavy bread doled out after the last Amen – perhaps thinking to make a little time with a plump and caring woman who had a little house and a paycheque from the mill – put up his hand and then inquired, "Now then, Miss, if you please, wot's all dis *ess-ay-vee-ee-deei*ng we does, de end of ebry chorus?"

My mother's ancestor, it is reported, put hand to mouth, eyes toward heaven, sought the air for answers and finally announced, "Why you dear twit, it's speakin' in tongues, that's wot it is, it's speakin' in tongues!"

After a kindly major had taken her aside later and explained the facts of life she sought out a free night school for the poor and wayward, quit the Sally Ann, got an education, married (rather late in life) a "readin'-writin' man" and with him began a line of avid scholars a goodly number of whom, by the third generation, became teachers or ministers or professors of such social conscience they had no time to write for scholarly journals. Jason Everest, therefore, had been destined by the will of his mother for a university career before ever he drew breath of life.

It was after I met the genus *Iguana* that "the things" started to visit. They were not simply the stuff of dreams. Dreams I had had, too many, ever since I could remember. They were populated always by creatures of the kind not seen in books. They were wearing harnesses and saddles, some of them, as though they served as beasts of burden. They lived in a land the colour of old sand. The terrain, as far as the dream-eye could see, was a mass of . . . well . . . minor protuberances that reminded one of anthills or – as it came to me later, once I had flown over the teeming seabird colonies off the coast of Labrador – the lime masses deposited by such a population.

The creatures of my earlier dreams were lizard-like, in some respects, but their eyes were the eyes of condemned men and their faces those of old women who have seen much too much. I awoke from such dreams with an unclear mind, and for days afterwards I would perform my duties at school and on the farm as though my life on Earth was some dream world and my real duties lay elsewhere.

"He seems so . . . so *distraught* somehow," I once heard my mother say. "He was so cheerful, as a child, and now . . ."

"Years ago," my father said. "That was years ago. He's a man now. Takes things a bit too seriously, p'rhaps. Preoccupied. All those books. Nose forever in 'em. Wait till seeding time comes around (or a pretty bit of fluff) and he'll soon pull out of it."

In point of fact, a young lady did come along. I was much attracted to her. I was reading eyes by then – the eyes of humans. The messages in the eyes of the Lacertilian creatures of my dreams still eluded me. We were at the university. She took all of the same labs I did. Whenever she was near I received, over the complete surface of the body, the speck-sparks of an electrical field mutually attractive to my own.

Whenever I looked at her a check-list went off in the left-hand side of the head. It listed her attributes: soft, shining hair, the colour of taffy left a bit over-long in the cooking pot; an odd, pale blue light shining always from large, deep amber eyes set in a small face with regular, rather nondescript features; a lithe boy's body; a certain toss of the head, when challenged, that reminded me of the spirited and sure-footed Jackie of my wild childhood rides. The consensus was delivered, in words, into the small compact "box" that lay in the middle of the head, just under the skull: *Plain, but bright/This one will do!*

Eventually, it transpired. I had just come back to university after missing nearly a full term. I had been needed on the farm, I told her. Actually, by then the presences were visiting me on a too-regular basis. The creatures I knew from my dreams. It was interesting, at first, to see them presented as some almost palpable "stuff" among the moonlight and shadows late at night in my room. They were the charges (perhaps the "steeds"?) of shadowy beings somewhat resembling humans but with only the vaguest suggestion of features or appendages – somewhat like misty Egyptian mummies. They were the colour of ancient sand.

They would drift in and out of the beige wallpaper towards pre-dawn and were as a consequence sometimes difficult to discern, except for the pale blue sun each wore at approximately the place where the human heart would lie. They "spoke" in the mind-language of ideas, but their thoughts seemed to be imprecisely presented (or imprecisely received by myself) and I much doubted the messages then.

My parents heard me carrying on conversations night after night, the summer the beings began to appear to me. My mother said I wasn't eating and, apparently, not sleeping either; my father said I looked "like death warmed over". I protested, but weakly; the mind seemed beset by a fog of some sort and it was difficult to disengage the appropriate words for something equivalent to "I feel fine!" from their pigeonholes inside the ever-expanding box-in-the-head.

The day the grain auger accepted three fingers from me as a penance for my disbelief in the presences, my parents took me, first, to Emergency at the nearest hospital, and then, blood still seeping through the bandages, to a psychiatrist in Winnipeg.

"Yes, yes, I *know* Hospitalization won't cover it," my father said, puffing his pipe now openly in the kitchen, "but at least no one else will know." I was sitting across the table from him, staring into a bowl of porridge. As the brown sugar on it melted it formed the face of one of the night visitors.

They had names by then. This one was Luke. Bringer of Light and Knowledge. Oh, definitely! The next afternoon I was on a psychiatrist's couch, two weeks later in a private institution "for paying guests", eight months later home with a certificate pronouncing "a sound cure" to be placed in my father's wallet where, presumably, it helped to fill the cavity formerly held by hundred dollar bills.

Somewhere in between there had been shock treatments. Luke for a long time persevered, in the manner of a Churchillian English bull dog, but eventually "he" too went the way of the other presences , of the harnessed and saddled lizards, of the old-sand country polka-dotted with grey-white "guano mounds", the way of the compelling pale blue sun.

My mother found many words to try to dissuade me from a return to my studies. ("You'll become *ill* again!" were the most-oft repeated.) My father's "Nonsense! He's sound as a dollar!" held sway. And I had no sooner set foot back on campus, it seemed, when Roxanne was there. And, with her, the presence, Luke.

"Rocks!" he shouted, into the box in the middle of the head. "Dangerous! Won't be allowed!"

The first night I tried to sleep with her . . . well, I *slept* with her. For Sandrah came that night for the first time. Unlike the others, her facial features were fairly apparent, most particularly the eyes. She delivered no words, she simply flowed into me as swiftly as air into a vacuum jar once the seal has been broken. I could feel her essence penetrate the body through its bloodstream to the veriest capillaries of appendages and brain.

Except for the crucial area. It became a cold and barren sea.

Roxanne had all the words to explain it. And furthermore, she said, it was the relationship itself that was important, not the biology. And she loved me enough to keep on trying, she repeated over and over. "And you love me," she said. "Don't you, Jason?"

"Of course," I said.

Fifteen years later, the grounds for divorce was a litany of my failure to "demonstrate any sincere human feeling whatsoever, even for his own progeny." The child, Luke. I moved to California. Purely at the behest of the presences. There

I found no dearth of the lizard species and a new career, for my curiosity about the *Iguanidae* led very quickly to an all–consuming interest that translated in a few years to being considered "the man who knows" when it came to lizards.

The presences left me. I never dreamed anymore. For twenty-three years, lizards were my life. Interviewers suggested, sometimes, I must be the happiest man in the world to be so taken up in work I loved and in a field where I was so respected.

"Oh, quite, quite," I said. I had begun an analysis of the phenomenon of feeling about that time. What, after all, *was* "happiness"? Was it this . . . this . . . *box*, this box of *quietude* I was in? I knew not discontent . . . yet, what was *content*? When I contemplated it I realized that I did not know what *love* was. Or how to do it. Or how to be it. Yet I supposed I loved.

For I had kept a picture of Roxanne on prominent display all these years.

She sent me pictures of the child, too, as he grew. He was a very *loving* person, she wrote, underlining heavily the telling word to make certain I did not miss the point. Over and over I told my mind: I *love* these two beings! I sent the support cheque promptly and regularly; the mind never once presented the possibility that I might stop doing so, and sometimes, now, I sensed the need to assure myself that meant that in some way I actually loved them.

My parents came to visit me often. My mother would turn Roxanne's picture face down on the mantel, first thing, when she supposed I wasn't looking, and she would ask coy questions about "lady friends" and suggest singles groups. My father would puff his pipe and say, "Leave the boy alone." I was about fifty then.

"I'm happy enough, Mother," I would say.

"What? Don't you miss Lukey? You *must* miss Lukey, Jason, very, very much!"

"Of course," I said. Out of the large picture window overlooking the park I was seeing, as though afloat, a drab country the colour of old sand, and lit by a pale blue sun. Its rays were directed towards me; I could see them; it was like a blue spotlight out of the night and I speculated that surely my parents must be able to see it too. I almost asked them. Then the blue light was penetrating the heart, the brain – those two centres at exactly the same instant – and briefly, ever so briefly, I felt intensely the feeling of yearning, of longing for I knew not what.

It was as though the heart and the mind had been placed in isolation from the rest of the body. Yet they had nowhere to go, nowhere to be. They were nothing but an idea now, separate and apart.

"Of *course*, I miss it!" I cried.

"Oh look, Edward," said my mother, "there are tears in his eyes, poor boy."

Thus alerted, I went immediately to the rather sophisticated laboratory that comprised the major area of the house and there took a sample of the tears for analysis later on. Unfortunately, the specimen was not adequately capped, and by the time my parents left the sample had dehydrated. As I could not rebuild it authentically I had to abandon the attempt.

On my sixtieth birthday the dreams began again. I saw the drab land, only this time I was bidden, by some non-worded process of mind, to sharply scrutinize a particular protuberance. As I watched, it opened as though a hatch were swung wide, and I caught a glimpse of a sudden radiance. I had only time to assess it as similar to a rather glorious display of aurora on a winter night in the northern parklands of Saskatchewan when it faded. The "hatch" had been swung to again, I supposed.

That night the presence Luke returned briefly. He made it known that I would be given a birthday present in the very near future. Three days later I received word that my parents had been in a fatal vehicle mishap on their way to the city. They'd meant to put the farm up for sale, neighbours told me later. If they got their price they were going to surprise me with the news and move to California to be near me.

While I was contemplating this turn of events, alone in the laboratory, the room began to fill with presences. There was a clamour of mind-messages, all of them the same: *Come home. Come home. Come home.*

The next day, I put all my Californian affairs in the hands of an agent, threw into the Landrover what personal effects I could gather together quickly, and headed for Saskatchewan. The first night home, lying wide awake in the familiar bed in the soft and silent darkness of my old room, I consciously solicited the presences. I acknowledged their existence. I called aloud for them. I begged them to appear.

It was Sandrah who came. I knew her at once though she had not presented herself to me since the night, some forty years ago, when I had first tried to come together with Roxanne. She came into me. She told me without words that she had come to take me home. The message surged through me: heart and brain and sinew pulsated with an energy that was electrical wholeness, that was rich rushing life-essence. That was Joy, unbounded and unending.

I could not bear, somehow, to take the steps to deliver myself of the body. Anything I contemplated seemed so untidy, somehow. So Sandrah agreed to stay.

For thirty-three years we have bided in joy together here on Earth, carried home each night, from the silver bed she composed for us, to the old and true homeland.

Now it is done. This holy night, we shall ride gladly the pale blue sun stream on the last, the final journey. Home.

AFTER WORDS

AFTER WORDS

After all's said and done, after all that a writer wants to say has been said, then she should be done. She should shut up and retire to a hermitage or a nunnery (or what passes for both or either nowadays) and raise flowers or Cain or chickens: be done with words in the head.

But if you are a writer who does not do your own writing, if you are a One who is really a schizophrenic Two-in-one – with a Writer Inside who is in direct contrast to yourself – why, then you know: what *you* want doesn't amount to a hill of beans; what *you* want doesn't count one breath's worth of wishing or whining; what *you* want doesn't mean one jot or one tittle against the words that The Writer Inside wants to say.

This will be a story-within-a-story. And, therefore – as any and every writer who has ever undergone a Saskatchewan Writers' Guild class will be screaming already: Why, oh why, would you put a story *within* a story; no, no, no, there is a rule about this and the rule says that you must begin a story at the story's *beginning*, there is to be no sneaking of it into a story that's already begun.

Against which ruling I shall avail myself of another writers' rule: There are no rules; if there are, they are there to be broken – you just better jolly well know why and how you did it, that's all!

And I do know why. At least, right now I do – by tomorrow the reason may have flown over the cuckoo's nest along with a few other of my ungainly cuckoos. But right now, I know the *why*. It is because I am sitting in a McDonald's in Wien – OK, Vienna. I have had the first coffee in two weeks that at least approximates the taste and texture of "home" coffee, rather than that of half a pound of burnt Colombian, ground fine, then stirred up with a (tiny) cup of hot water, some double-strength Dutch chocolate, a good jag of cardamom, some salt, vanilla and a glob of imitation cream – and all for less than $4 Canadian – so count your four stomachs or your good luck (the first,if you are a cow; the second, a homesick Canadian) if they don't all come up together three minutes after that heavenly scented chocolatey-brown earth goes down.

Homesickness is not the story. *Heimweg*, it is called in schoolbook German; *Heimweh*, it stands in a rather moving poem written about his own homeland – lost many years ago to Poland – by a seventh-order cousin on my mother's side, a poet-painter-friend I had not met until after I was sixty years old and had been sent to the Germany he lives in today by that unsatisfiable Writer Inside who claims there are no rules to the writing game except those *she* sets out for me.

So I am not homesick. I have dealt with that in the same way I have dealt with everything life has presented since the night the infamous "Fort San Ghost" spoke into the ear of a Canadian poet a message for me and so trapped me forever into the rule-making Soul-of-me who also passes as The Writer Inside and by virtue of whom the very hairs of my head are numbered, by virtue of whom I breathe and weed potatoes and saw firewood upon demand. And take dictation for her/Its stories.

Ah yes, that Fort San Ghost. The "presence" who made himself/itself known at a writers' retreat on the old hospital grounds where Saskatchewan "beat TB" (since it couldn't beat the drought or the banks or the weather) a good long while ago, which is somewhat the way Saskatchewanians count their history. But that's another story, that Fort San Ghost story, and perhaps sometime I shall accept the discipline to tell what it did to me.

That is not to the point just now, nor is the *Heimweh*, the sickness of mourning for a home one is absent from. When that feeling surfaces, I immediately place it (sometimes I *hurl* it, with the force of a fair overhand girls' team pitch) into the hands of Spirit. That *doesn't* mean the catechismed Spirit of the holy catholic Lutheran Church; it means the original, never-ending, we've all got it every single second, life-giving electrical Energy that created all that ever was, and is, and will be.

It is somehow important to define terms, even in a typical McDonald's in present-day awful old Vienna, with three different kinds of German penetrating the concentration that writing demands of those who have agreed to be channellers of the words of The Writer Inside. It is important to define terms, let's make no mistake about that.

So then, what is this all about? It is not about the Fort San Ghost and it is not about *Heimweh*. Maybe it's about the Confessional, I don't know. I've been in enough churches now, in my time in German-speaking Europe, to have confessed all the sins of 4,449 lives, if only I could remember them, those many sins – or even a few more of the lives.

I think that is somehow it. In the last three days, while I have been covering the countries – giving EuRail a run for its money, so to speak – three different people have said to me in three different dialects of German: Aren't you brave! Travelling around Europe all alone. And at *your* age!

How do you say, courteously, in a language that, while it feels somehow "good" and somehow "right", is not your mother tongue and cannot, therefore, be so easily manipulated to spare the feelings of others: If I were *not* at this atrociously advanced age I would have yielded to good sense and I wouldn't be here at all! If I were *not* afflicted with the crazy-quilt illness of senility I would be safe at home reading books and watching "Coronation Street" and eating white bread and dark chocolate and drinking *good* coffee boiled in an open pan thirty seconds by the clock, one teaspoon of coffee to a whole bloody panful of water, thank you very much!

How do you tell a fellow traveller of even your mother tongue that only a few years ago you were of the firm belief that anyone who heard voices in the head was on pretty shaky ground, but that anyone who would actually *do* what some still, small voice inside told one to do, was not only fairly crazy, but downright dangerous?

How do you smile (out of crazy eyes?) when you confess you are in a strange country alone because your head told you to go and to be there?

So. Anyway, I am sitting in a McDonald's – the one that same crazy head had told me would be here if I would only get the Sam Hill out of the long hot money-changers' line in Vienna's very rude and angry railway stationhouse. The still, small voice gets louder when the world around us is too loud for its comfort. And it was fairly roaring when it reminded me we were here to find "the real people", and if I would only do as bade we would find not only kindly folk but a McDonald's. (In "our" personal and private "head language" that meant COFFEE!!!)

About exclamation marks, by the by: A Saskatchewan professor of English Literature told me once, on a paper of mine he was grading, that exclamation marks are the sign of schoolgirl writing. I was forty-seven – and felt seven when he told me that, but those exclamation marks are to stand, by jingies, even supposing this journal entry ever becomes a short (maybe not so short) story, and that is that!

This is not really a journal entry, either. Journal entries go into the coil scribbler right side up. The writing that may form part of a manuscript goes into the same coil scribbler, but from the rear door, let's say, so it is upside down if you leaf to that section from the journal section. It is a good system for the traveller who needs to travel light because she is travelling alone at a severely advanced age (and therefore makes sure *she* swings the bulky searing-orange packsack up on the overhead racks of EuRail's trains despite offers from younger stalwart male passengers). There is a large Canada-flag sticker on the packsack. Let those young men go home and tell their mothers at suppertime: *Die alte Kanadierin war sehr robust!* (With an exclamation mark or two in the voice!)

This may not be a journal entry, but right now it is at least a report. Or maybe research notes. But anyway, The Writer Inside, serving double duty as The Not-So-Still Small Voice Inside, got me out of the money-changers' line, whereupon I saw a sign that coaxed me to come along to the Austrian post office and they/it would be happy to change my money for me. I followed the signs (it was a little like a treasure hunt) and eked that out with inquiries in bad but sincere German (and was answered kindly, for now I was among "the real people", right?). And got money changed in less time and for less surcharge than at the railway station.

Now the voice was silent. Non-existent. I settled in to dream-mooch along the streets, following my nose in the way that children without a care in the world do, when all at once my head was jerked sideways by The Silent One and there was McDonald's. I was about ready to miss it completely.

While waiting for coffee to be ordered and presented, T.S.S.V. got very busy inside and told me: *Awful new old Vienna shall be a true short story and you shall write it here.* When the coffee came and I wandered doorwards with it instead, She brought in old Kaiser Wilhelm's martial guards, I think, to help her holler: *SIT!*

I sat. At a corner table in a not very clean McDonald's, by "the real Germany's" standards (to tell the truth, not by Saskatchewan standards, either), with the good coffee long gone down the alimentary track, at twelve Austrian schillings which, being mostly paper bills, gives you the horrible feeling at first that you have just paid twelve dollars for a fifty-cent cup of brew.

I wrote. It wasn't dictation, for the most part; it was me pouring out. Eventually I grew aware that the room was filling with German voices; just behind me a child's voice was saying "*Hah*-lo, Oma! *Hah*-lo, Oma!" in the musical way of all the children who speak the German tongue from babyhood, in whichever of its myriad (and often, weird) dialects.

The left-hand mind of me began announcing: I've got to get out of here; I've overstayed by two cups of coffee too much, especially considering it included a visit to a WC that did not cost the fierce flush of anger arising from the realization that one is required to pay money each time a sixty-year-old bladder requires some flushing out.

But the left-hand mind does not rule the day here; the right-hand mind does. That is where dwells The Writer Inside (and, perhaps Soul, too – at least I am often "told" so by that stubborn inner head of mine, I just refuse to believe it). The right-hand mind is in charge, so, in spite of the long conditioning that warns me that an honourable consumer uses the time and place of a business in accordance with the money spent there, I sit and I write, albeit more quickly, real hen-scratching – so that it will be a quick mind, indeed, that deciphers it all when I get safely home.

It is like this: After the age of sixty, if you have a head full of angels so full of love for you that they require you to tell them every thought, holding back nothing; after the age of sixty, if you are so alone that you have finally got it all together for the first time in 4,447 lives; if, after the age of sixty, you have found your Self in all its myriad of facets and are still alive (and maybe even kicking), then you are finally set to report, honestly, honestly, on the Self you have, to this stage in your growingness, become.

Of course, it doesn't wear a halo, this Self.

As for example: As soon as you begin to wear on your face the lines of a grandmother, everyone assumes you are the typical stereotype of the indefatigable *oma* with the smudge of flour on the cheek and an apple pie tantalizing even the wood-stove oven that is harbouring it to golden brown in its cosy innards. And so one is sought out, even in utterly complicated languages, and bound about with the fish-line of: Ah, but you remind me so much of my dear grandmama! Or some such equivalent in the language of the solicitor. A halo slips noticeably just then.

So with the young Czech who thrust his way into my first-class railway compartment after I had the curtains drawn, my shoes off, and the seats on "my" side already made into a bed. I had had "a day and a half and then some" as my Uncle Bill used to say, in the last twenty-four hours, and I was in hopes of having the compartment to myself.

I am travelling first class, I hasten to explain – given the fact that I am travelling at all by the good grace of the Saskatchewan Arts Board – not because I cheerfully fling grant money to the four winds, but because the sellers of EuRail passes back home will not dispense you a second-class one: even begging and/or pleading advanced age will not get a foreigner a second-class ticket on EuRail. You will often have to actually *travel* second class, but that, like the Fort San Ghost, is another story.

It is not only definitions we must set out here, it seems, in this story that is really more than just a story, but the finer cobwebby threads in the Code of Saskatchewan Ethics. I mean to say, of course, apart from that which operates the general run of legislatures back home.

So, this young man thrust his way into "my" compartment. And ensconced himself in and on the three seats across from me which were, though not yet made into a bed, a very short distance from unshod feet that had seen neither bathtub nor river water for three days, only the damndamndamn wet warm rain that had soaked them (and, therefore, of course, also the neat little red Italian leather shoes I'd got five years ago for two dollars at the Prince Albert Sally Ann where a sign says GOD LOVES YOU and the bargains in even new shoes prove He loves at least your budget enough to be very kind to it, the shoes I had been taking such precious care of because they were so pretty and so sociable to the feet).

So there we were: my body, including its three-day-old feet; the shoes, no longer pretty; and a stranger. So naturally, I got my feet out of his face in a hurry though so tired I could hardly think in English, let alone in *Deutsch* – or Hungarian or Lithuanian or Lutheran or whatever it was this guy was speaking. I am hurrying here even more now – in spite of having replenished the coffee twice to assuage the guilt of overusing one of (Mrs.) McDonald's Viennese tables – because I do not relish reporting this incident, I know it.

And this fellow was carrying along two dictionaries, a big one and a small one. He had a determined voice and a determinedly friendly manner (at twenty minutes short of midnight) and besides that he had a whole lot of questions he seemed determined to get answers to (from me, more's the pity). He also had some sentences written in German on a paper.

As, *zum Beispiel*: *Ich habe kein Geld. Ich hab Geld.*

He pointed with a determined forefinger to the latter. He gave me to understand, via body language and bits of German and English and lots of some other language(s) that, not only did he have *Geld*, he had lots of it, and would like to buy American dollars from me.

As I remember it, his final solicitation was : Oo-ess fur Kroner, OK? As I remember it, he had flung open the curtains when he had first burst in, but he got up and closed the curtains when he began to talk about money. I do not believe that impression is a manufacture of the creative mind, although, goodness knows, it is getting pretty good at exactly that sort of thing the last few years or so.

Well, thank goodness I hadn't any. Any Oo-ess dollars or even any Kroners. (For I did get to thinking, later, maybe I'd misunderstood and it was Kroner he wanted to *buy*. But somehow, I don't think so.)

All the same, I had slipped into the old Lutheran pattern of willing entrapment: here was a soul in trouble and who was I to be too tired to discipline myself to communicate with and maybe to comfort him. The words flew. The dictionaries, his and mine, flew ferociously, too, back and forth. Mine was tiny. I loved it. It had cost 50 pfg at a second-hand bookshop somewhere in the Schwarzwald. It had a leather cover and was very old; old enough to be badly out of date, I presume, for it was tough going with the young Czech and I don't mind saying so.

Over an hour later I began pleading, in body language and in German and English and (I hoped) a few words of Czech, my need for sleep: Sleep! *Schlaf!* Beddy-bye! A-a-ah! See? I lay back on my "bed" and curled an arm over the face. I was sure I didn't have to act out "dead-on-my-feet" because my body was shouting it. I closed the eyes. No, that's wrong; they slammed shut of their own accord. God, that felt good!

"Aha!" he said. (I am pretty sure Aha! means Aha! in every language known to man.) I opened an eye. He was digging in his carry-all again. His wasn't old and searing-orange and borrowed from a son-in-law, like mine; his was new and terribly efficient with lots of zippers and pockets and compartments. He took out a magazine. "Aha?" he said again, this time as a question, pointing to the magazine, to me, to the magazine.

I guess he wants me to read it, I supposed. (And I may add here there was no help from the marvellously wordy Writer Inside while all this was going on. There was, though, at different times during the "encounter", a series of definite *feelings*. Right then, somewhere in the ether about me, somebody or something was having a jolly good chuckle, and what was so funny, I'd have liked to know.)

I sat up and took the magazine. It was a girlie one. In Swiss. He said the word for Swiss. I myself never got beyond the pictures. (The positions seem to be the same in Swiss, it seems useful to report.) He took the magazine back, paged in it rapidly. He passed it back. It showed two people . . . well, *sleeping*. Maybe.

I grabbed my things – nearly forgetting the sodden red shoes (I hadn't any others) – and went to look for another compartment. Half an hour later (I'd spent it watching my watch and watching the curtains of the compartment against their being parted by interested hands) the train stopped and a sweet grandmotherly-looking soul with no flour smudge on the cheek slammed the door open and after a surprised Ah! (at least it wasn't an *Aha!*) gave me to know, in excellent and sympathetic German, that *she* had the room "engaged". I'd certainly EuRailed it like a mad university student enough by then to recognize the word for "engaged".

Well, I hadn't seen the "Engaged" card on the compartment window, but hey, when you've just been shown the breasts and whatevers of an entire hatchery of Swiss chicks the eyes may be a bit glazed and the brain not as electronically fine-tuned, let us say, as a fine-tuned, old-fashioned war.

In any case, I had to go back to the talkative young man, there was no place "unengaged" left to go.

To leave in the first place had taken some doing. Years of doing. What I am trying to say is, it took me sixty years to work my way painfully to the Self who can say, under the circumstances: Ich . . . go now! You . . . *du . . . bleib da!* I mean it, Buster! So, to go back in would mean . . . what? . . . in any kind of language.

He was sleeping like a baby. I prayed I wouldn't wake him up. It worked: you don't snore if you don't sleep. The lovely monotony of train wheels which generally works like a mother's lullaby for me produced, instead, the I'll-never-sleep-again effects of a rock band in its earnest, learning stage.

Just as well. Five times in three hours we were awakened by Austrians on the Austrian section of this train's journey into night: train tickets, passports, train tickets, passports. In West Germany I'd never once been asked for my passport, but, as the saying seems to be: You're in Austria now.

I'm not sure it's to the point here, but I've just been reminded of something else my fellow traveller seemed to have spelled out on his piece of Helpful Phrases scribble paper. Things to Say and How to Say Them. It was: *Wo ist deiner Mann*? He had seemed very pleased when I made a sad face, drew tears on my cheeks, pointed to the ground and then up "towards heaven" (for good measure drawing an imaginary halo around my own head and then flapping angelic wings to help him get the drift). Joe Story doesn't spend a whole lot of time hanging around heaven, if you ask me; he seems to have a heck of a lot better time of it helping my Soul to make me do things I do not really want to do – such as go to Europe to see if I can learn to dream in German and then remember it.

I think I remember also that then the young man took up both his dictionaries at once and flipped pages and perused them and then came up with: *Du*, me. *Kanada*. Work. I can't remember who or what changed the subject but when the subject of *meiner Mann* came up rather determinedly a couple of times again I simply said over and over that I didn't understand.

When I think back on it now, I expect I should have been glad about the frequent clip-clopping of heels in the foyer, the brisk banging entry into the compartment, the unnecessarily loud requests for Pess-port! Pessport! (no please about it). Police *and* border officials, besides train personnel, and all of them interested in our pess-ports. There were grey uniforms with black on them here and there and with stripes and stars and medals and medallions. There was now and again a gun and twice the young man was prodded awake with a night stick.

I did not like that. I was going to say so, but someone from just inside the head, left-hand, said: *Keep your trap shut!* And then there was a whir and whirl of sounds and pictures and smells and feelings – all seemingly dished out by the *right*-hand mind – and it told me most certainly that this is how it all starts: with silence.

The words were on my tongue: Don't *do* that! let me wake him for you! But the words remained unsaid, and I had to know myself then for a One who, after sixty, would not make a new crusade inside myself to create the Self who will say, easily and as a matter of course, to those who come in the night: Don't *do* that!

It was a night for lessons, I suppose. One thing I learned was how clearly one hears and sees and interprets when the Self sees itself threatened. I marvelled at how easily the young man slept after each interruption and I denied it when the idea once presented itself that perhaps he was pretending. One thing for sure, when the night stick brought him to the surface in quite a groggy state it was interesting to note how much his German seemed to have improved, for he spoke quickly and easily then.

Well, that's the way I saw it at the time. Now, having recorded it so, I am reminded that sometimes when I am busily congratulating myself for having spoken excellent German during an encounter with those born to it, there suddenly springs to mind Christel's story about her French.

Christel is one of the two "cousins" to have come my way during the sojourn to the land of my mother's ancestors. Once she went with a friend to visit a French family. Christel loves people and loves to make them feel at ease and she has, furthermore, spent very little time on the reincarnational wheel bound to silence; let us put it that way. Coming away from the visit she said to the friend, "Oh, I feel so good about how well I spoke French tonight."

Said the friend, "Christel, my dear, I'm afraid you forgot again to listen to your *French*, you listened only to the joy of speaking it."

Maybe it's the same with me and my understanding of German, but all the same, my watchful mind said the young man spoke German too well the times he was awakened with the night stick.

Another thing. Four times at least he was told: You have a second-class ticket; you are in a first-class carriage; go *that* way two more cars. (Body language included.) Four times he said, Ya, ya, ya; four times he began to gather up his things; four times, as soon as the official (or the plural thereof) had departed, he closed the curtains and lay down again and slept.

By the light of morning I saw his hair was quite grey and there were some lines in his face, and I was very disappointed.

So,thus far, this story that is not really a story, seems to be suggesting some sort of theme or lesson. Maybe two: (1) it is my pathway, this time around, to analyze and inspect this Self I am constantly becoming; to do so honestly in any given circumstance, and then not chastise or judge or condemn, and (2) I have a need to accept the discipline of mind to grant the same principle to others.

So far I would not give myself a lot of medals.

I left the "young man" still sleeping. He had not put the seats into sleeping position again, but he slept in sitting position in the seat next to the window. I stood in the foyer to watch beautiful and green Austria pass by; to admire – even to love – its vineyards and gardens and orchards checker-boarding the green, green lower hills, the forests a smoky blue-green in the upper hills farther away.

The Oben Wald, the map says. *Oben* means 'above' and *Wald* is 'forest', of course. 'Woods', really. Villages nestle here and there in the valleys, their houses red-roofed, the churches with needle spires decorated in coloured patterns outlined in silver – three churches allotted per village, it seems.

Later in the morning we are joined in the compartment by a couple who are going on holiday to Budapest. He is in a wheelchair. They are roughly forty-five, and very loving to each other. Kind to me, too, and to the grey-haired man, looking less young as the morning gets older, when he finally wakes up.

They are from Lenz, the newcomers. Many people, they say, go to Budapest on holiday. It costs a pittance compared to what it costs at home. I should come too; they'd be glad to have me, for they've rented a full house for three weeks. We calculate its cost in Canadian. The man is very quick that way. It would be about a hundred and fifty dollars. She runs out to ask someone if I would need a visa. I get caught up in it all and do the same thing in the other direction. No one is interested and, perhaps because it is nearly the end of the run, no one is very polite.

When the train has pulled into the station it is a long, long walk from the platform to the station proper, yet there are no baggage carts set out at regular intervals as there are in Germany. I have become accustomed to the thoughtful way of doing things. The Germans themselves seem to see it simply as efficiency. They talk of a well-ordered society, but I have appreciated it as thoughtfulness. Maybe motive doesn't matter, so long as the interests of ordinary people going about the business of living are served. On the other hand, as soon as those words are on paper, I know that is not the way I want it to be.

As I come through the main entrance a woman approaches me. She is about forty, forty-five. She comes too close and then stops me. I don't like it. "Do you need a room for the night?" she asks. I know she is not one of the "angels" the System of All Things has stationed for me here and there along the route: Austria so far has been utterly devoid of angels. There is an odd smell about her. There was a time I didn't notice such things.

All the same, someone speaking from my mouth says, "How much?"

"How long do you intend to stay?"

"Only one night."

"Oh no, I need someone for two nights. Two nights for six hundred schillings. It should be twice that but I'll let you have it for six hundred, you won't do better anywhere, let me tell you."

"I would rather get back on the train and sleep there." Where is the One who once would have trotted out all the rationales, the explanations, the creative whys and wherefores to let her down easily? Perhaps it's just that I don't have time. I have one day of "being in Vienna" and must, in the careful way of Virgoans, check out the train and platform number and so on for the departure later that night. The familiar German billboards with the yellow placards for the departing train schedules and the white ones for arrivals are nowhere to be seen. I ask someone with INFORMATION printed on his neat firm-crowned cap. He yells in dialect a lot of stuff that amounts to: You have on your paper when it goes, what more do you want? Come back at six o'clock and ask somebody then!

I yell back, "In Germany *we* are used to efficiency and *that* means letting people know *kindly* what it is they want to know!"

Another large step backward on the road to enlightenment and I don't even give a good damn!

Well then, I wasn't trapped there forever, of course. Under the premise that one might as well have the game as well as the name of backslider I went stomping around until I found another uniform whose head was also wearing one of the INFORMATION caps.

The first thing I said to him was in English: I bet they had them on sale, right?

I then proceeded to explain, with utter disregard for grammar and syntax but with great care taken in the degree of hauteur that framed the request, that I was taking a train that night for Zurich and I expected him to tell me exactly when and where I would be able to board its first-class carriages. He was to tell me slowly and kindly or else write it on a piece of paper for me.

He looked at me. He took the paper and wrote the details on it. I was satisfied. He looked at me again, perhaps wondering if I meant to require him to salute next, and weighing the pros and cons.

I'm going out on the street now, to meet the real Vienna. This nice cheery woman, on my way here, when I asked her if there was a *Bäckerai* nearby, said, "You are a lucky traveller, the best one in Vienna is just across the street from where we stand. Shall I go with you?" I shall go there next.

I may not see too many monuments and castles and the innards of cathedrals here today, but I don't suppose they've changed much since the first time I was here.

The bright young woman who poured my last cup of McDonald's coffee told me I speak German much better, at least, than *her* grandma speaks English; and one thing certain, her grandma would never head out for Canada alone. "What a brave thing," she said. "And at your age!"

Well all I ask, at my age, is that when I get back to Vienna's main train station tonight, Train # E126 will leave Platform #5 at 19:35 and not one second later. And I can pretty well guarantee, if there are any Viennese waltzes whistling inside the head it will be some sort of sneaky cosmic joke from The Writer Inside or from some Fellow Traveller from the Etheric World who's along for the laughs.

I'll tell him to bugger off and not come back unless he's wearing an Austrian train worker's INFORMATION hat. Put up or shut up. After sixty, you can take only so much enlightenment in any three days by the calendar, and you have to learn how to handle these "helpers" inside your head.